'Do you still think there was no one. . .special?' Robert asked quietly, and Fenella shook her head miserably.

'I've told you, I haven't the faintest idea. But how could there have been? I surely couldn't have forgotten. . .not something as important as that.'

'Perhaps,' he said, and his voice sounded remote, as if the subject was distasteful, 'whoever it was wasn't so important after all. Perhaps you *want* to forget him. Or perhaps you should accept that there was no one.'

'Yes. I think I should.' She glanced at Robert, at the clear lines of his face. . . At the body that would be tall if he ever stood upright again, lean and strong like an athlete's.

'I'm sorry,' she said in a low voice. 'You must think I'm being melodramatic. Especially when I—I can get up and walk away, and you're stuck in——'

'You needn't say it,' he said in a clipped voice.

Books you will enjoy
by NICOLA WEST

A WOMAN'S PLACE

TV producer Marc Tyrell made it clear that
he would not work with a prickly woman,
and he expected Jan to swallow her prin-
ciples and acknowledge that he was the boss.
But Jan had other ideas—after all, hadn't
men had it all their own way for too long?

LAST GOODBYE

When Jenna married Dair Adams, the
wealthy, rugged farmer who'd swept her off
her feet, she thought it would be the hap-
piest day of her life. The last thing she
expected was for Dair to shatter her dreams
immediately after the ceremony!

FORGOTTEN LOVE

BY

NICOLA WEST

MILLS & BOON LIMITED
ETON HOUSE   18–24 PARADISE ROAD
RICHMOND   SURREY   TW9 1SR

*First published in Great Britain 1991
by Mills & Boon Limited*

© Nicola West 1991

*Australian copyright 1991
Philippine copyright 1991
This edition 1991*

ISBN 0 263 77067 2

*Set in 10½ on 12 pt Linotron Times
01-9104-51402
Typeset in Great Britain by Centracet, Cambridge
Made and printed in Great Britain*

CHAPTER ONE

IT WAS a game such as Fenella Sutcliffe had never seen before. She knew that, even as she wondered how she knew. For what part of her brain could tell her this, when it could tell her so little else?

The players were of a different breed too. Especially the dark man, whose silver-grey eyes pierced her like twin swords as he passed and then swept by, concentrating once more on the game he was playing with such ferocious determination. She found herself watching him, almost willing him to look at her again even though his glance had seemed to drive directly into her heart—a frightening feeling, and especially for Fenella. Had she seen him before? Had they ever met, known each other? There was no way of telling.

But if they *had* met, had known each other in that other life. . .could she really have forgotten? Could she have forgotten the impact of those silver eyes, the sudden gathering of the straight black brows as he looked into her face, the strength in the firm lips and jaw? Could she have forgotten that indefinable magnetism radiating from him, even as he shot past in pursuit of the ball that another player had dropped?

No. It was impossible. Whatever else might have been wiped from her memory, this man couldn't have gone too. *Surely*. . .

Fenella passed a trembling hand over her brow. These moments when memory seemed so close, yet proved still to be so elusive, were almost the worst aspect of what had happened to her. When was it all going to end? When was she going to be fit to face the world again?

She tightened her hands into fists, as if taking a grip on her emotions, her fear. This certainly wasn't the way to go about recovering. Determined not to give way yet again, she stared again at the players, her expression almost fierce as her own eyes, grey as a dove's wing, followed the man with the silver glance.

This hospital which her doctor, Sam Whitman, had brought her to, had turned out to be a pleasant place, larger than the convalescent home where Fenella had spent the last weeks. Its greatest difference, she had seen as soon as they arrived, was in the patients—all disabled in some way, many in wheelchairs, some learning to cope with artificial limbs.

Fenella looked at them and felt a rush of shame. How could she wallow in self-pity when she was strong and whole, with all the faculties of sight, hearing and speech, while others were having to face life minus an important part of their bodies? As Sam had shown her round the wards and the sunny gardens, she had passed people who wheeled themselves rapidly along the paths, a knot of young men who were vying with each other to show off their prowess with artificial arms. All of them grinning and cheerful, facing up to their new lives with courage—the kind of courage she hadn't even tried to cultivate.

She tried to concentrate her attention on the game. You couldn't call it football, though Sam had told her the rules were more or less the same. It was really more like rugby, with the players carrying the ball and passing it to each other as they swooped up and down the pitch. All the players were in wheelchairs; some of them, she knew, doomed to stay there for life.

Fenella found herself watching again for the dark-haired man. He would have been tall if he had been able to stand, she thought with a pang. He shot past her now with barely a glance, intent on capturing the ball, and she followed him with her eyes, disturbed by what she saw, yet unable to look away. There was something about him, something vital, something that plucked at a nerve deep within her. . . What could have happened to bring him here? A car accident? Or had he been injured while doing something adventurous like mountaineering, or skiing? He looked the sort. . .and it was unfair. So unfair. . . She found her eyes hot with sudden tears and bit her lip.

'What is it, Fenella?' Sam asked quietly, and she shook her head and brushed the tears away.

'I was just wondering why I've been making so much fuss all these past weeks. There's nothing the matter with me, nothing at all. It's just a kind of hysteria—because I'm scared to face the truth, whatever it is.' She spoke angrily. 'These people—they've faced their truth. They're getting on with their lives. Why can't I, Sam? Why can't I remember it and put it all behind me, and get on with *my* life?'

'There's no accounting for the tricks the mind can play,' he said. 'Don't fight it, Fenella. But it needn't stop you from putting it behind you—getting on with life. You can do that. I think you're ready to do it—aren't you?'

'Yes,' she said, and looked again at the dark, grey-eyed man who had paused at the far end of the lawn and appeared to be watching her. 'Yes, I think I am.'

Back at the convalescent home, Fenella moved restlessly to the window of her room and stared down at the garden where people walked or sat in the sun. Some were almost ready to leave, looking forward to going home; others had only recently arrived. She knew their family backgrounds, their histories, their hopes and their fears.

But nobody knew hers.

Stabbed by the familiar sharp pain, she turned away from the window and tried to think of something else. Something pleasant. . . But there was so little, so little to draw upon. Her memories were so few, so brief, and they were all concerned with the hospital where, it seemed to her, she had been born. 'Born' six weeks ago, aged twenty-six, small and dark, with grey eyes that were large with fright and bewilderment, staring out at a world that she didn't know.

They hadn't known at first about her amnesia. They couldn't have known, of course, until she had regained consciousness, until the injury to her head had been almost healed and her sleeping brain had at last consented to allow her to wake from the dreams which were her refuge. But even then, when she'd opened her eyes and looked around the small, clean room with its pale walls and pretty curtains, it had not allowed her to wake fully. And the extent of its determination to stay asleep had transpired only gradually, as they had begun to question her and she to question them.

'Where am I?'

It was the stock question when someone woke from unconsciousness. The nurse who had been with her then, watching every flicker of her eyelids, keeping an eye on temperature, pulse and brain patterns, had come swiftly to her side, smiling a professional smile.

'You're in hospital. How do you feel?'

Fenella looked at her uncertainly. She moved her head a little. 'I think I feel all right. Why am I here?'

The girl hesitated. 'You had an accident. Would you like a drink?' She held a cup to Fenella's lips. 'Don't try to talk too much. Sister will want to see you—she'll answer your questions.'

But Sister didn't answer any questions. Alerted by the nurse that the patient in Room Six had woken at last, she came at once, clearly pleased by the development. Fenella had the impression that she'd been unconscious for quite a long time. How long? An hour—a day—a week? Nobody would say.

The doctor told her when he came next day and sat down beside her bed, drawing his chair close as if for a long talk. By then, she was feeling stronger, had managed to eat some breakfast, and her mind was dizzy with alarm—an alarm she had seen mirrored in the faces of the nurses, however well they tried to conceal it.

'I can't remember who I am!' she burst out as soon as he came into the room. 'I can't remember anything about myself. It's as if I'd just arrived on earth, able to talk and think, knowing what to *do*—but nothing else. As if I'd just been born!'

The doctor looked down at her and laid his hand on her arm. She was quivering with panic, like a tiny bird trapped by a cat. She stared up at him, trying to gauge the expression on his wrinkled, monkey's face, trying to read hope and reassurance in his eyes, but saw only a gravity and compassion which frightened her even more.

'What's happened to me?' she cried. 'Why can't I remember? Who *am* I?'

He nodded at the Sister to leave them, and sat down. He held her hand between both of his and she felt the warmth flowing into her. He was trying to give her strength, strength to face whatever horrors lay unrecognised in her mind, but she didn't want to face them, she didn't need that. She just needed to know who she was, what her life had been. . .

'Tell me what you do remember,' he said.

Fenella shook her head. 'Nothing! I don't know *anything*.' It was a cry torn from her heart. 'I told you, it's as if my life began here in this bed when I woke yesterday. I don't even know how old I am.'

'Surely the nurses——?'

'Oh, they've told me things, yes—that my name's Fenella Sutcliffe, that I'm twenty-six years old, my birthday's in May so I've only just had it—but that's all. And I don't *know* it, inside myself. They could tell me I'm Queen Victoria or Meryl Streep, and I wouldn't know the difference.'

'Except that you presumably do know you're not either of those two ladies,' he suggested, and she met his eyes and relaxed slightly.

'Yes, I do know that. I know who I'm not.' A flicker of irony touched her voice. 'So all we have to do is go through the whole world and find out who I'm not and then. . .but I've told you, they say they know who I am. *I'm* the one who doesn't.'

'Yes,' he said thoughtfully. 'Well, what's happened to you isn't really uncommon, you know. You've had a nasty blow to your head and either that or the circumstances in which it happened are preventing you from remembering any details about yourself—your own life. Apart from that, your memory probably isn't affected. After all, you know about Queen Victoria and Meryl Streep——'

'Thank you,' she said bitterly. 'That's all I really need to get me through the rest of my life, isn't it?'

'I'm sorry. I didn't mean to sound like that. I know this is a dreadful situation for you. But it's sure to improve——'

'Is it?' She stared at him and felt a twinge of fear, unexpected as a sudden toothache.

'Almost certainly,' he said with belated caution. 'Nearly everybody who suffers from this kind of amnesia recovers from it eventually. It may take time, but——'

'Time?' she pounced. 'What do you mean by *time*? A few days—a year? Longer than that?' She stared at him with wide eyes the colour of water, huge storm-driven lakes in her pale face. 'And will I remember everything?' Again she knew that twinge of fear. 'Everything?' she repeated in a whisper.

The doctor looked at her thoughtfully, noting the trembling that had begun again, the pallor that was to do with more than a wound that had almost healed while she lay in her coma.

'It depends partly on why you've forgotten,' he said slowly. 'It may have little to do with your injury. It may be that you don't want to remember——'

'But why shouldn't I want to remember who I am?'

He smiled faintly. 'The brain isn't always quite so selective. If something happened to you that it thinks is better buried, it may bury quite a few other things along with it. In your case, everything that happened to you before.' He stood up, still holding her hand. 'Fenella, the best thing you can do now is rest. Try not to worry about all this. You can't force memory—it will come back of its own accord, perhaps all at once, perhaps gradually.'

'Or perhaps not at all,' she said quietly, and saw the answer in his eyes before he turned away.

It was only after he had gone that she realised he had not told her his name. But perhaps that was because he had felt embarrassed at knowing it, when she knew so little about herself.

And she still knew very little more, Fenella thought as she stared down from the window at the people in the garden. It had become almost a routine, this going over in her mind what she had been told about herself. Told—not remembered. Was it really any use to go through it all again? Wouldn't she be better off to put her past where it belonged—in the past?

But she couldn't help it. It was like an addiction. And—who knew?—one day it might trigger off some tiny thought, some small memory, a chink of light that might open the darkened windows in her mind.

She counted her small store of knowledge off on her fingers.

Fenella Sutcliffe. Aged twenty-six. Living in a flat in North London, which she had apparently bought outright only three months ago. Employed by a temping agency, working as a secretary wherever they sent her; so far she'd had four jobs with them, none lasting more than two or three weeks, covering for girls away on holiday or off sick. No friends, no one who knew her socially.

No hint as to where she had come from before buying that London flat.

If she knew what had happened to her, how she had been injured—would that help? She flinched from the answer and the monkey-faced Dr Whitman, whom she was learning to call Sam, had regarded her thoughtfully when they had discussed it and said it was better not to press that particular line. It might, indeed, bring it all back—but, if her mind wasn't ready for the knowledge, it could do more harm than good. Better to let it happen naturally, in its own good time.

'That's all very well for you,' she told him pettishly. 'You're not the one without a past. You can't begin to imagine what it's like.' And the weak, easy tears began to flow again.

'Perhaps not. But I do try. And you don't really want me to tell you what happened, do you?' He waited while she searched her mind and began to shake with the terror that flooded in whenever she questioned too far. 'You see? Don't rush it, my dear. Let it take its time.'

'But supposing I *never* remember?' she cried in anguish, and he took her hand again, giving her the strength he could always transmit.

'I think you have to consider that possibility,' he said quietly. 'And simply start living your life again. There really wouldn't be anything else for you to do. But I don't believe it will come to that,' he added quickly as she began to protest. 'One day, I believe you'll remember. When your brain considers you strong enough to——'

'Strong enough to what?' She stared at him, willing him to answer, but he remained silent and after a few moments she supplied the answer for herself. 'Strong enough to cope with whatever it was that happened to me. That's what you're saying, isn't it?' And she knew, as the trembling began again, that she wasn't strong enough. And might never be.

Whatever it was, the trauma she had been through seemed to have condemned her to beginning life at twenty-six. With no family, no friends, no memories.

No past.

Fenella moved away from the window. The people down there looked carefree, almost as if they were on holiday. They were getting better, looking forward to taking up their own lives again. . . She fought angrily against the self-pity she was always afraid would invade her, returned to the life she had been told she'd led. Surely *something* would help her to remember. . .?

They told her she had grown up in a small country town in Suffolk until her parents had moved when she was eighteen and had just left school. She had worked as a librarian until her parents had been killed together in a road accident in Canada. What Fenella had done then remained a mystery. People had moved on, it was difficult to trace any friends, and she didn't appear to have kept in touch with anyone.

'In fact, I don't seem to have made any impact at all,' she had remarked wryly as Sam Whitman sat with her one sunny afternoon. 'Obviously the ideal candidate for vanishing without trace.'

'Don't say that.' His seamed face gathered a few more wrinkles as he frowned at her. 'You're an attractive girl, Fenella. The problem is your having moved to London so recently. Obviously you've had jobs; the secretarial agency was more than satisfied with your work.' He paused. 'I really think you'd be better off to leave all this questioning, Fenella. I've told you before, let it come back naturally. It's the best way.'

'But I must have *some* friends,' she said unhappily. 'Why hasn't anyone missed me? Why doesn't anyone come looking—to my flat, for instance? Didn't I give anyone my address?'

'Perhaps you didn't,' he said quietly. 'Perhaps you *wanted* to vanish, Fenella.'

Shocked, she caught her breath and stared at him. *Wanted* to vanish? Could that really be the answer? And if so—why?

What secret could be hidden in her past that had made her want to cut all her old ties, whatever they were? That made her want to hide it even from herself?

Was it something she had done—or something someone else had done to her?

Again, she felt the terror grip her, felt the shaking begin. And knew that Sam was right. She had to stop this questioning. She had to leave the past where it was and go on into the future. Alone.

She had been almost ready to leave the convalescent home, her physical wounds healed even though her mind was still haunted by the memories she could not recall, when Sam had told her he wanted to take her out for the day. 'I have to visit another hospital on the way, I'm afraid,' he said, but shook his head reassuringly when she looked at him in alarm. No, they didn't think she needed any more treatment. He was going for quite another reason.

'You think I'm going to see something that'll bring it back,' she said, and felt herself draw back. 'Sam, I'm not sure——'

'Now, don't start panicking,' he said at once. 'I don't think anything of the sort is likely to happen. Don't think about it, Fenella. It's just a day out, all right? I have to see someone there, but you needn't worry about it. You're coming along for the ride and

a pleasant lunch in a little country inn I know. I want
to see how you shape up to the big world before we
let you loose.'

She looked at him with suspicion, but his face was
as bland as the hundred tiny wrinkles would allow.

'All right. If you're sure nothing will happen.'

'I'm sure,' he said, but she wasn't quite convinced.
Something was going on. But she had trusted Sam
Whitman from that first morning, when he had sat
beside her bed and held her hand, and she trusted
him now. Whatever was going to happen, it wasn't
something she need fear.

Now, gazing down from her window and remembering the ball game, she felt again that Sam had
had some purpose in taking her to that other hospital. And she remembered again the lean man with
the black hair whose presence dominated the grassy
lawn, whose trapped body vibrated with an energy
and vigour which it seemed impossible to contain in
the cage of a wheelchair.

There had been something vital in that meeting,
she was sure. Something that would, in some as yet
undefined way, affect the rest of her life.

The next day, Sam told her about the job. He told
her in the office at the convalescent home, making it
a more formal discussion than they had been accustomed to having. During the past few weeks, they
had become friends, meeting more casually than as
doctor and patient, their talks conducted over a cup
of tea or coffee. Sitting in the office, facing him,
made her realise that there was still a formal side to
their relationship, that Sam expected her to take his

advice, that soon she would be leaving this place and would no longer have him to turn to and lean upon.

The thought brought a tremor of apprehension.

'A job?' she repeated doubtfully. 'But I don't know what I can do.'

'You're a good secretary, we know that. And you have library qualifications—you'd be a good secretary to a writer. Able to help with research, that kind of thing.'

Fenella felt a quiver of interest. Research. . .yes, perhaps. . . 'Is that what you've got for me?' she asked. 'Sam, are you thinking of setting up in competition with the agency?'

He grinned. 'I've got enough to do, being a doctor! No, this is just something I happen to know about. Another patient, an old friend of mine as a matter of fact. Just about to leave hospital, but unfortunately he's not ambulant—can't walk. Sorry, of course you understand, I'm being patronising.' He was talking quickly, as if he wanted to gloss over something, and Fenella watched him curiously. Just what was in Sam's mind that prevented him from meeting her eyes? 'Anyway, this man's a historian, writes erudite books about European history, and he needs someone who can—literally—do his leg-work for him. It would involve living in—he's got a rather pleasant house in the Cotswolds—and it sounds just the thing for you. Get you back into the world without having to try to cope with the hurly-burly of finding an ordinary job, coping with your home and everything.' He stopped and looked at her. 'Well—you can think it over, can't you? No need to decide straight away.'

Fenella gazed at him. On the face of it, it did sound a good idea. But she still had the feeling that there was more to it than met the eye.

'Just what are you up to, Sam?' she asked, and then she knew. 'This friend of yours—would he be a patient at the hospital we went to yesterday?'

'Well, yes, as it happens, he is.' The doctor looked uncomfortable and toyed with a pen lying on the desk.

'As it happens! Sam, you're as transparent as that window. You took me there to be inspected, didn't you? So that this man could see me and decide whether he liked the idea of my living in his house and doing his legwork! But why? Why should he want me—another lame dog? Wouldn't he rather have someone properly fit and well, someone who could be trusted to go out and not forget to come back?' And she repeated her question. 'Just what are you up to, Sam? You might as well tell me.'

'All right,' he said. 'I admit I engineered it. But I knew he wanted someone—and I knew you. What's wrong with putting the two of you together? If you don't like the idea, you have only to say no.'

'And how am I to know if I don't like it?' she asked. 'I need to meet this man before I can make any decision. Surely you can see that, Sam.'

He relaxed suddenly, his monkey's face creasing into a grin. 'Certainly I can, Fenella. And you can meet him any time you like.' He paused, and his grin grew a little wider. 'Now, if you care to.'

'Now?' She stared at him. 'You mean he's here? Now?'

'He is. He wanted to come over straight away. I

wanted time to prepare you, but he wouldn't have it. Said if you had time to think, you might refuse. I knew you wouldn't—you're not the terrified mouse you were a few weeks ago. But he came anyway. He's outside now, on the lawn. You can go and meet him at once—if that's what you want.'

Felicity gazed at him. Slowly, she stood up and crossed to the french window. She looked out at the terrace and her eyes rested on the wheelchair which stood with its back to her, facing across the wide lawn to the fields that stretched away from the convalescent home.

She knew instantly who it was. She could visualise without having to see the thick black hair springing from the well-shaped head, the eyes as grey as hammered steel, the firm, compressed mouth. She could remember the long, lean body, still athletically muscled yet tragically useless. She could feel the shiver of apprehension, the sense of undisclosed peril, that had touched her yesterday as she watched the wheelchairs speeding across the lawns in pursuit of a football.

Forgetting Sam Whitman, she opened the door and stepped out on to the terrace. She walked across the broad flags until she reached the wheelchair. As she approached, it turned so that its occupant faced her.

Fenella stopped. Her eyes met the unwavering gaze of the man who sat trapped by his disability, a man who she knew had never been accustomed to illness, had probably not had so much as a common cold for years. She felt the magnetism in those eyes, the power of a personality that demanded to range the world and was forced to confine itself to a set of wheels. She felt a shock of fear, a sense that if she were wise she would turn now and put as much distance as possible between her and this man who watched her so impassively.

She took a breath. But the words never came.

'I'm Robert Milburn,' the man in the wheelchair said, and there was an odd note in his voice, a note she couldn't analyse. 'I take it Sam's told you about the job I'm offering. Will—will you think about it?'

It was that slight hesitation which was Fenella's undoing. That tiny hint of an apprehension that could, impossible though it might seem, be almost as great as her own. And she wondered again just what it must be like to lose the use of your body when it should be expected to be—*had* been—in its prime. Particularly such a strong and virile body as this man had clearly enjoyed.

'At least,' he said, 'you could give me a try.'

Something in his voice twanged at her mind and for a brief instant, gone as soon as it had touched her, she had a sensation of familiarity—as if she had known this man before. She caught her breath, staring at him—but no, it was impossible. He was looking at her now with no more than non-committal enquiry. . .or was he? Was there something else in those cool eyes—something that was deeply suppressed but smouldered deep inside, ready to flare up at an unexpected moment. . .?

Fenella touched her dry lips with her tongue. The fear was still beating at her heart, even while the magnetism continued to draw her closer. She put a hand to her cheek and felt the fingers tremble against

her skin. She wanted to say no. She steeled herself
to say no.

'Yes,' her voice said. 'I'll come.' And she knew
that whatever danger this man represented it was
something she had to face.

CHAPTER TWO

ROBERT MILBURN'S house was on the outskirts of
Winchcombe, one of the prettiest towns in the
Cotswolds, near the edge of the ancient park that
surrounded its pride and joy, Sudeley Castle. In the
wooded grounds, you could believe yourself to be in
deep country, miles from any human habitation.

Fenella arrived with Sam on a fine Saturday
towards the end of June. Why he should be expected
to ferry her around was beyond her understanding,
but he had dismissed her remonstrations lightly,
declaring that both she and Robert had been so
troublesome that he wanted to see for himself that
they were safely off the premises of any hospital he
had connections with. . . 'Besides, it's a long time
since I came down to Robert's place. And he owes
me a free tea.'

Fenella sighed and gave in. She had already
allowed him to take her to the London flat to collect
some more clothes, and had been aware of his
unobtrusive observation as she moved hesitantly
about, opening cupboards, choosing skirts and
dresses as if she had never seen them before, sorting
through sweaters and blouses that were strange to
her, feeling as guilty as if she were rifling through
some other girl's possessions.

'I feel as if she might come in at any moment,' she

confessed, looking up to find his eyes on her. 'The girl who lives here. The real Fenella Sutcliffe.'

'You don't believe you're the real Fenella, then?'

Fenella shrugged. 'How can I? You've told me I am, and I trust you, so it must be true. But in myself—no. She's no more real to me than—than if you said I was Marilyn Monroe. Or anyone. It's just a name.'

He nodded. 'A name you've spent twenty-six years growing into. It's a lot of time to make up.'

'I suppose I'll get used to it.' She surveyed the packed suitcases. 'I don't think I need take any more than that. Professor Milburn won't be having smart parties, will he?' She looked doubtfully at the two cocktail dresses that still hung in the wardrobe. 'I seem to have had quite an interesting social life.' She looked at him in sudden despair. 'So why doesn't anyone remember me? Didn't I have any friends?'

'Presumably they're from your pre-London days,' Sam said, and she nodded sadly.

'I thought there might be some post. . .' But there hadn't been. No envelopes had come through the door apart from bills and a letter or two from the solicitor, about the buying of the London flat. And the solicitor had already been approached. He had known nothing of Miss Sutcliffe before she had bought the flat, and, since she had apparently had no previous property to dispose of, knew no previous address. Neither did her bank, apart from the lodgings where she had stayed while the purchase was going through.

'It really is as if I just sprang fully grown from

nowhere,' she said. 'I don't understand it. . . It's as if I'd already lost the years, since my parents died, before I even had the accident.'

Now, they were approaching Robert Milburn's house, secluded in its own grounds, sheltered from the world by its garden and its trees. And Fenella felt the tension rise in her and wondered again why she had ever agreed to come to this place.

She thought again of the afternoon she had spent with Robert Milburn in the grounds of the convalescent home. They had talked about themselves—he seemed to know all about her, or as much as anyone could know. He didn't question her about it and she thought that had had a good deal to do with her decision. Having to explain to people, over and over again, that she had no memory, had been one of the most daunting aspects of going out into the world again. Robert Milburn accepted it as just another disability, not so very different from his own.

He told her about himself. An Oxford don—why did people always suppose academics to be elderly and stuffy?—he had made a name for himself in his analyses of European history and the books he had written tracing the influences of eighteenth- and nineteenth-century history upon the wars and disruptions of the twentieth. He was now engaged on a book concerning various great sieges—from the biblical story of Jericho to the Siege of Paris in 1870 and, finally, the Siege of Leningrad in 1941.

'I need someone to help with the research,' he said. 'I've got a lot of the necessary books and contacts, of course—but there'll be visits to the

British Library and possibly a few other places to make as well. Do you think you could manage that?'

The British Library, Fenella thought, and the words had a ring about them that struck her as familiar as well as exciting. It was a place she had visited before, she felt sure; she would feel at home there.

'Yes, I believe I could,' she said slowly. 'I think I'd enjoy it. But——'

'I wouldn't expect you to do anything you didn't feel up to coping with,' he said. His eyes were on hers, intent and searching, and she realised suddenly that they were almost silver. Silver eyes. . . A brightness hovered momentarily at the edge of her mind, but, when she turned to face it, it had gone. She looked back at him and felt again that strange, unnerving mixture of attraction and fear. Why should she fear him? Why did she have this strange, fleeting feeling of familiarity?

'How did you know about me?' she asked suddenly. 'What made you think I'd be right for this job?'

'Oh, I was talking to Sam one day—griping about the deal life had handed me.' His mouth twisted wryly. 'That was before I'd looked around and seen just how lucky I was. They say there's always someone worse off than yourself. . .they're damned right as far as I'm concerned, though I think some of the poor devils I've met since the—since my accident—might have difficulty in applying it to their lives. Anyway, I told Sam I needed another pair of legs to use while mine were mending and he thought of you. I told him he ought to make a charge, but he said it all came free on the NHS.'

Fenella looked at him. The mild joke passed her by; she was thinking of something he had said.

'While your legs are mending? So—you will. . .'

'Get better? I certainly intend to.' Robert Milburn's mouth and eyes looked grim. 'I'm damned if I'm going to stay cooped up in this contraption for the rest of my life!' His tone was as grim as his expression now, filled with unyielding determination. 'I'll walk again within the year, or know the reason why.' He gave her a bright, sardonic glance. 'Being my amanuensis won't be a lifetime's occupation, I'm afraid.'

There was an odd note in his voice as he said those words, and something else in his eyes, something Fenella couldn't fathom. But she didn't have time to ponder on it. She was too caught up by the power of his determination. She had no doubt whatever that he would do exactly as he said. A year from now, he would be walking, and not on sticks. He would be striding as tall and as athletic as he had ever been. He would be climbing, too, conquering mountains as he had conquered his injuries, skiing, swimming—whatever he chose to do, this man would be able to do it.

And, if he could do all that, couldn't she conquer her own particular obstacles? Couldn't she face whatever demon lay hidden in her mind—and regain her memory?

It was that moment that finally dispelled all doubts in Fenella's mind. Robert Milburn might represent danger of some kind—and of what kind she had no real idea—but he also represented a means of regaining what she had lost, by his own example, his own determination to regain his lost ability. It was an opportunity she would not be given again, and she knew that she couldn't afford to let it pass her by.

She didn't look ahead at the day when Robert would be independent again, no longer needing her services. Since waking in hospital that morning so many weeks ago—a lifetime ago—Fenella had learned to live one day at a time. The past did not exist. The future was unknown.

There was only the present. Only *now*.

'Good afternoon, miss, sir.' The woman who came to the door set in the mellow golden Cotswold stone wall was stout, grey-haired, with a kindly face. 'Dr Whitman, it's nice to see you again. And you must be Miss Sutcliffe.'

Sam smiled at the woman and lifted Fenella's suitcases out of the car. 'It's good to be here. Fenella, this is Robert's housekeeper, Mrs Bennett. I suppose he's here, is he?'

'Yes, sir. He's having some physiotherapy just now, but he'll be finished soon and tea will be ready in the small drawing-room. I'll show you that first, before I show you Miss Sutcliffe's room, then you can come down as soon as you're ready.' She led them through the front door and into a square wood-panelled hall. 'What we call the small drawing-room is through here.' Fenella looked past her at a fairly large, comfortable-looking room furnished with large armchairs and sofas. She wondered what size the large drawing-room must be, if this was the small one, and why anyone should need two anyway. . . 'Your room is on the first floor,' the housekeeper added, and Fenella and Sam turned to follow her up the curving staircase.

As manor houses went, Cowleaze wasn't particularly big, Fenella decided later. But on that first afternoon it seemed enormous. And her own room took her breath away. Situated at the front of the house, it looked straight out across the lawns and woods at the towering battlements of the castle, with the tumbled grey roofs of the town just beyond. It was a spacious room, decorated in pale green and gold, the wide bed covered with a billowing white duvet covered in broderie anglaise; there was room for a table and chair, as well as a small sofa, and from one corner a door led into her own private bathroom with a separate shower.

'Well, you'll be comfortable enough here,' Sam remarked as she gazed around in awe. 'Looks as though Robert means to treat you right, anyway.' He grinned at Mrs Bennett's scandalised expression, and took the housekeeper's arm. 'Let's go down and see how that tea's coming along,' he said encouragingly. 'I think Miss Sutcliffe needs a few minutes to get accustomed to the idea of being here.'

Left alone, Fenella stood quite still, gazing around her. She had never expected anything quite like this. As an employee, already being generously paid, she had anticipated a modest room somewhere at the back. This was a room that would be offered to some honoured guest—and, once again, she felt a twinge of unease. There was something about this job, this whole situation, that didn't ring quite true. Something she felt she ought to know. . .if only she could put her finger on it.

If only she could remember. . .

She shook herself and turned briskly to the door. This was nonsense—she was letting her disability become an obsession. Clearly, regaining her memory would be of no use in solving the puzzle of Robert Milburn. They had never met before. If they had, he would have said so—and he had never given the slightest indication that it might be so.

That feeling she had about him—the feeling of danger that seemed to go hand in hand with the magnetic attraction he had for her, and that odd feeling of familiarity, as if they had known each other in another life—was just her mind playing tricks on her.

As if it had not already played quite enough.

Robert Milburn was already in the small drawing-room when she came downstairs, and Sam was pouring what looked like at least his second cup of tea.

'Oh, I'm sorry,' Fenella said, hurrying in. 'I didn't realise——'

Robert waved a dismissive hand. 'Nothing to be sorry for. Tea's an as-and-when feast here. This is John, who looks after me.' Fenella jumped a little, startled, as a man she had not noticed rose from a chair and smiled shyly at her. 'He gives me my physio, punches and pummels me a bit and generally does all the hauling and heaving that's necessary for a man in my condition.' The tone was ironic, as if

Robert was training himself not to feel bitter but had not yet reached the stage of full acceptance. As he was determined not to, Fenella thought. 'John, this is Fenella, who will do all the intellectual bits. Between the three of us, we ought to make one passable historian.'

'Plus one very attractive young woman and a young man, both with brains and lives of their own,' Sam observed through a mouthful of fruit cake, and Robert gave him a wry glance.

'All right. Point taken. It's obviously one of the faults of the recently disabled to consider themselves the centre of the universe. Or this particular one, anyway. I hope you'll both keep me in order.'

'I think you'll keep yourself in order,' Fenella said demurely, accepting a cup of tea from Sam. 'After all, if you have enough determination to get yourself walking again, a simple thing like self-discipline should present no problem.'

Robert's eyebrows rose and Sam laughed.

'That's right, Fenella! Don't let him get away with anything. I've known this man for years—been waiting all his life for the chance to play the spoilt child. Now—I'll have to be on my way. Work to do.' He set down his cup and stood up. 'See me out, Fenella?'

She cast a quick glance at Robert in his wheel-chair, wondering if he resented the suggestion that it was too much trouble for him to see his own guest to the door. But Robert merely nodded and waved one hand. Fenella followed Sam from the room and stopped at the front door.

'Thank you for bringing me, Sam.' Now that he

was going, she felt suddenly bereft. He had been a
rock for her to lean on during those frightening days
when she had first realised what had happened to
her, when she had struggled to regain even the
tiniest scrap of memory, during the lonely hours
when she had slowly come to terms with the loss of
her youth and the knowledge that she might never
regain it. Now he was going, and she would be
alone. She didn't know when she might see him
again—perhaps never. And she found herself looking into a bleak and terrifying abyss in which only
Robert Milburn knew the truth about her—and he
frightened her almost as much as the abyss.

What was she doing here? Why had she agreed to
come?

'It's all right.' Sam's voice reached her through a
wave of panic. 'You're all right, Fenella. There's
nothing to worry about.'

She found she had her eyes closed, and opened
them to look at him. 'How can you be sure?' The
words came in a whisper.

'Because I know you pretty well by now.' His
voice was gentle, strong. 'And I know Robert too.
You'll be all right, Fenella. You can cope with
whatever happens. Remember—you *can* cope.
You're strong enough.'

She took a deep breath. 'Sam—will I see you
again?'

'I'm sure you will. Robert's asked me to come for
a weekend, very soon.' He grinned his monkey grin.
'He's as uncertain as you are, you see! Does that
make you feel any better?'

It shouldn't have, since it was Robert's strength

that had drawn her here. But somehow, in that moment, it did help to know that he too had his uncertainties, his moments of doubt. That he too still needed Sam's support.

'You'll be good for each other,' Sam told her now. He looked as if he wanted to say more, then decided against it. Drawing her swiftly towards him, he dropped a brief kiss on her hair and then stepped away.

Fenella watched his car disappear down the drive and turned to go back into the house. She wondered what it was he'd been going to say. She had a feeling it was something important—something that could have begun to clear away the cobwebs in her mind.

Did Sam hold the key to her mind? And could it somehow have something to do with Robert—with that strange sensation she still experienced of attraction mixed with danger, a fear that set her heart thumping yet wasn't quite enough to make her want to run away?

She remembered a poster that had been pasted to the wall of one of the rooms in the convalescent home, which had read: TODAY IS THE FIRST DAY OF THE REST OF YOUR LIFE. It had always struck a bitterly ironic note with her. But now it seemed real, and true.

She took a deep breath and went back to the room where Robert waited for her. . .to begin the rest of her life.

Robert was alone in the room. He glanced up impatiently as she came in and said, 'I was beginning to think you'd changed your mind and gone back to London with Sam.'

His tone was unexpectedly grumpy, and Fenella looked at him in surprise. She felt a little nettled—not least because for a moment she had been almost tempted to do just that—and answered sharply,

'If I'd decided to do that, I would at least have let you know.'

'Hmm,' he said non-committally, and she felt a small flare of anger. Dismayed, she sat down and looked at the tea-tray.

'Do you want another cup?'

'What? Oh—no. You have some if you want, though.'

My, she thought, we are being the gracious host. Silently, she poured milk and tea, and took a slice of cake. Her heart was jerking uncomfortably and she realised that this was the first time they had been truly alone together. She stole a look at him through her lashes. He was staring at a magazine, but he hadn't turned a page yet and she suspected he wasn't reading it at all. What was the matter with him? Was he regretting having brought her here?

'My room's lovely,' she said at last, politely. 'Much nicer than I expected.'

'What did you imagine I'd give you, a broom cupboard? Or the servant's quarters?'

'No, of course not, but——'

'You're going to be here for some time, so naturally you should have a decent room,' he went on. 'I don't anticipate entertaining any overnight guests, anyway.'

'Oh—I thought Sam said. . .'

'Said what?'

'That you'd invited him to come for a weekend soon,' she said lamely. 'Perhaps I was mistaken, though. I could have——'

'Oh, *Sam*,' Robert said dismissively. 'Yes, he may come. But I wouldn't give him the best room in the house. I doubt if he'd even notice.'

'So he'll get the broom cupboard,' Fenella suggested mischievously, and Robert's impatient glance caught her just as her twitching lips broke into a smile. For a moment, he stared at her, his expression unreadable, then, almost reluctantly, he grinned back and Fenella felt suddenly light-hearted and happy.

He reached out a hand towards her and her heart skidded. Tentatively, she put her own into it and felt his strong fingers close warmly around hers.

'Keep doing that,' he said quietly.

'Doing what?'

'Laughing. Smiling. Making jokes.' He hesitated, then added, 'It makes things better for me. For us both.'

Fenella was silent for a moment. Then she said, 'I have a feeling that's what I used to be like. Always laughing at silly jokes. But since the. . .accident. . . I haven't seen much to laugh at.'

'Then try to now. You're right. You. . .must have been the sort to see fun in so much. You must regain that—it's a wonderful gift. It can't have been destroyed.'

She gave him a glance of surprise. His voice had deepened, losing its casual note and becoming intense, almost passionate. It was as if it really mattered to him, she thought in wonder. But how could it? She was nothing to him—an employee, battered like himself, but nothing more. Perhaps it was the fact that they were both casualties that gave him a fellow-feeling towards her.

At least he seemed to have lost his grumpiness. And how could she blame him for feeling bad-tempered, when a small thing like seeing a guest out of the front door could bring home to him his helpless condition? Yes, he could have wheeled himself out—but the doorways were narrow, the floors uneven, and it would have been difficult. And his daily life must be filled with such bitter little reminders. Just as hers was, when she thought idly about the past and came up hard against the solid brick wall that surrounded her memory.

Suddenly conscious that her hand was still resting in his, she made to withdraw her fingers, but his instantly tightened.

'Professor Milburn——'

'Robert,' he said quietly. 'We're going to be living here together. You must call me Robert.'

'Robert. . .' She said breathlessly. 'Please. . . I want to drink my tea.'

He released her hand at once and Fenella felt her colour rise as she picked up her cup. The feeling of his fingers still burned around hers. It was strange, exciting, disturbing, and yet as if at some other time, in another place—another life—he had held her hand like that before. It was the sensation she'd had earlier, up in the bedroom, yet Robert had not even been with her then. It was as if his magnetism was powerful enough to reach her even through the old stone walls of the house.

She shivered a little. What was it about this man that compelled her to his side, yet at the same time made her quiver with sudden, tiny spurts of terror? If only she knew.

If only she could remember.

Fenella shook herself. As far as Robert Milburn was concerned, there was nothing to remember. They had never met before her accident, nor before his. She wondered briefly which had occurred first. She had been told as little about Robert's accident as about her own, and she could not ask. It didn't affect the main issue, anyway, which was why she felt this odd sense of familiarity. As if she had been held by those fingers before, as if she had felt the strength of his arms, the passion of his mouth. . .

She set down her cup so sharply that it clashed against the saucer. Her cake lay untasted on her plate. She stared at it, wondering why she had taken it.

'Do you really remember nothing about your life before your. . .accident?' he asked quietly.

Fenella caught her breath. It was the first time he had referred directly to her loss of memory, the first time he had probed even a little. Her eyes misted and she bent her head, shaking it slightly. She was conscious of him leaning a little closer; she could feel his nearness like something palpable.

'No little jokes?' he persisted. 'No memories of things you might have shared—with someone special, perhaps? No feeling that you're missing someone—someone you might have loved?'

Fenella raised her head and stared at him. The agony in her heart darkened her eyes to pewter. Briefly, she wondered why she didn't feel resentment at this probing, why she didn't hate Robert Milburn for making her face up to a pain she had tried to evade. Again, she shook her head and then, at the expression on his face, the words tumbled from her lips.

'I don't remember *anything*,' she cried. 'Nothing at all—I don't even know whether I've ever been in love. Except that I must have been, surely, at twenty-six. There must have been someone—some time. But if there was—whoever he was—I've forgotten him along with everyone else.' She covered her face with her hands and repeated what she'd said to Sam, what she'd told herself through so many sleepless nights. 'But there couldn't have been, could there—because he would surely have looked for me? He would have found me—even if I didn't recognise him.' Slowly, she lowered her hands and looked at Robert with a hopelessness that brought a twist of expression to his face. 'And surely I *would* have recognised him? Wouldn't I?'

There was a moment's silence. Then Robert said, very quietly, 'I don't know, Fenella. Perhaps—perhaps not. And I'm sorry—I shouldn't have asked. It's obviously too painful for you just yet. But——' he leaned closer again and captured her fingers in his, holding them so that she could feel their warmth and their strength '—when you do feel ready to talk, I'll be here, Fenella. You'll remember that, won't you?'

She gazed at him, trying to read the expression in his darkened eyes; then, slowly, she nodded.

'I'll remember.'

He held her look for a moment, then released her fingers and said, so gently that his voice brought tears stinging to her eyes, 'Why don't you go up to your room now and unpack? You must be tired.' He hesitated, then added, 'And you don't have to spend all your free time with me, anyway. Make your own life here, Fenella. Make friends in the town. You only have to work for a short time each day—you're not in gaol here.'

She felt her breath quicken. The thought of venturing out alone into the town was a little more than she was ready for. If he could have come with her. . .but that was impossible. Or was it?

'Don't you want to go out?' she asked. 'Perhaps we could——'

'No!' His voice was sharp. 'I'm not being taken out for walks in my pushchair, like a baby. I'll go when I can go on my own two feet and not before. But there's nothing to stop you exploring. It's pleasant enough countryside hereabouts.'

'Yes.' Feeling suddenly drained and knowing that she couldn't bear any more of these sudden swings of mood, she stood up. 'I think I'll do as you suggest,' she said quietly. 'I'll go and unpack. And then perhaps I'll go for a walk in the grounds. I don't really feel like going much further at the moment. What time does Mrs Bennett like to serve dinner?'

'Dinner?' He looked at her as if he had never heard of such a thing. 'Oh—about seven-thirty, I

suppose.' He spoke almost as if he were a guest here
himself, she thought in exasperation. Didn't he have
any interest in the way his home was run? 'Why
don't you go and ask her?' he added. 'She's probably
in the kitchen now.'

'I'll take the tea things out.' Fenella lifted the tray
and hesitated. 'Is—is there anything I can do for you
before I go?'

'No, thanks.' He looked at her for a moment and
she caught a strange expression in his eyes, as if he
wanted to say more. She felt a tingle in her spine, a
sudden wash of emotion, and the tray rattled in her
hands. Shaken and disturbed, she turned abruptly
and left the room.

Out in the hall, she leaned for a moment against
the wall, fighting for her composure. What *was* it
about this man? Why should she feel that she knew
him, and not merely as an acquaintance, but on
some deeper level; that somewhere hidden in her
heart and mind, too deeply buried to be revealed,
was an intimate knowledge of him?

It couldn't be. If they had met before, he would
have said so—why shouldn't he? And surely he
would have triggered her memory? Such a powerful
emotion as he seemed to ignite in her could surely
not have been overruled by a mind that was simply
afraid to face up to an accident.

Sharply, Fenella moved away from the wall and
made for the door which must lead into the kitchen.
Sam had warned her of this—that straining too hard
to remember might make her mind play odd tricks.
This was no more than one of those tricks, brought
on by the knowledge that she and Robert Milburn

were to live in close proximity for an unspecified length of time. It could be nothing else.

But, as she carried the tea-tray into the big, sunny kitchen, Fenella was conscious still of that surge of emotion. And of the way her heart had kicked when Robert Milburn had looked deep into her eyes and seemed to want to say something more.

CHAPTER THREE

'Do you want a few days to acclimatise yourself,' Robert asked at dinner that evening, 'or would you rather begin work straight away?'

Fenella looked at him. He had brought his wheelchair up to the head of the long table and she sat on his right, facing the open window. On the long window-seat stood a bowl of sweet peas, and outside she could see the garden, brilliant with roses.

'I'm ready to start whenever you want,' she said. 'I'm not sure exactly what you want me to do, though. You talked about research.'

'Yes. Well, at the moment there isn't too much. The real legwork comes later on, but for what I'm doing at present I've got most of my books and papers here. I thought it would be a good idea if we worked together for a while, so that you can get used to the way I like to do things, and the kind of information I'll be needing. It'll be more secretarial work to begin with—I hope you don't mind.'

His tone was oddly formal, as if he had decided that it would be a mistake to allow their relationship to become too friendly; as if he was determined to remain on a strictly employer-employee basis. Well, that suits me, Fenella thought, remembering that disturbing look in his eyes. I'm not ready for anything else.

Perhaps she never would be now. For until you

knew yourself how could you begin to know anyone else?

She had a sudden feeling of loss that was almost too much to bear, as a question that she had previously allowed into her mind only at night came abruptly to stab at her. Had she, in that other, lost life, been in love? Had there been a man who cared for her, cherished her, and whom she loved in return? And, if so, where was he now? Why hadn't he searched for her, written, telephoned, come to that flat in London that had seemed so alien when she and Sam had gone there to collect her clothes?

The inescapable conclusion was that there had been no one. That she had been totally alone—without family, without friends, without a lover. But why?

I'm not the kind of person to be alone, Fenella thought. I like people—I *know* I do.

She became aware that Robert was watching her, and felt her colour rise. Hastily, she helped herself at random to more salad, and tried to remember what he had asked her. Something about secretarial work.

'No, I don't mind at all. I think it's a good idea. What sort of hours do you work?'

'Much the same as anyone else—all day. Writing books is just a job, you know, like any other. At least, writing my kind of book is. I don't wait for inspiration.' His tone was dry. 'Unfortunately, my present condition has forced a few changes to my timetable. I breakfast alone—I'm not fit to talk to before nine anyway. You can come to your own arrangements with Mrs Bennett over yours. Then I do an hour's physio with John, so I won't be able to start until ten most mornings. We work until one, have a light lunch, then go on from two till four or five. I may do some more in the evenings, but I won't expect you to do that, naturally. In fact, for the first few days it might be an idea for you just to read through a few of my books, to get the feel of my work.' His glance held a measure of humour. 'You'll probably find them stupefyingly dull.'

'I'm sure I won't,' Fenella denied at once. 'I love history.' She stopped abruptly. That was something else she hadn't known until the words came out of her mind. 'I'd love to read your books,' she added, her voice trembling very slightly.

He gave her a sharp glance. 'You haven't read any before?'

'I don't know!' It came like a cry of pain. 'How can I?' She laid down her knife and fork and raised a hand to her forehead. 'I don't know what I've read. I don't know *anything*—anything about myself. I've lost it all.'

'Is that really so?' He looked at her reflectively, then said in a casual tone, 'So where will we find Toad of Toad Hall?'

'*The Wind in the Willows*,' she said instantly, and stared at him. 'Oh!'

'Alice?'

'*In Wonderland*. But——'

'Tiny Tim?'

'*A Christmas Carol*. But, Robert, this doesn't prove anything. Those were all books I read as a child——'

'Which proves that all your childhood knowledge

is intact. And, as we know, so is a good deal of your adult experience. You can type, for instance. In fact, everything that's at all useful to you has been retained. So why worry so much about the rest?'

Fenella stared at him. 'But I don't remember anything. Oh, I know the answers to those questions—and probably lots of others. But what good does that do me? There's so much I've lost. My parents—I don't have any memory of them. Can you imagine what that feels like? All the childhood memories: holidays together, days in the garden, Christmases, being helped with my homework, discussing things with them; their advice, standards, the jokes we must have shared—it's gone, all of it, gone. Can't you understand what that does to me?' She stared down at her plate, feeling the tears hot in her eyes. 'And the years since they died—what have I been doing all that time? Wasn't there anyone who was special to me? Wasn't there anyone I loved? It's like some dreadful void, and I'm so terrified that I'll fall into it again and be lost forever.'

Her last words echoed in the silent room. She leaned her head on her hand and stared hopelessly out of the window, afraid to look at the man who sat in his wheelchair only a foot or two away from her. It was the first time she had ever given real vent to her feelings and she felt sick and shaken.

'Do you still think there was no one. . .special?' he asked quietly, and she shook her head miserably.

'I've told you, I haven't the faintest idea. But how could there have been? I surely couldn't have forgotten. . .not something as important as that.'

'Perhaps,' he said, and his voice sounded remote,

as if the subject was distasteful, 'whoever it was wasn't so important after all. Perhaps you *want* to forget him. Or perhaps you should accept that there was no one.'

'Yes. I think I should.' But the thought brought an added sadness. As if she had lost something precious, something she'd held very dear.

She glanced at Robert, at the clear lines of his face, the firm mouth, the straight black brows, the silver eyes. At the body that would be tall if he ever stood upright again, lean and strong like an athlete's.

'I'm sorry,' she said in a low voice. 'You must think I'm being melodramatic. Especially when I—I can get up and walk away, and you're stuck in——'

'You needn't say it,' he said in a clipped voice. 'And the two things are hardly comparable. But we both have to come to terms with what's happened. We have to endure what we've got—or make up our minds to get over it.'

'You've decided you're going to walk again. But I can't decide to get my memory back—it doesn't work like that.'

'No, and I don't think you should.' His eyes were on her, with that dark, intent look she found so disturbing. 'Look, something's happened to you that your mind has decided you don't need to know about. Unfortunately, wiping it out has also wiped out a lot more. But if your own subconscious, if that's the right term, thinks you're better off knowing nothing than knowing that one thing—well, why argue with it? Why not accept that it's right and start life from here? Isn't that what Sam's advised you to do? And the other doctors you've seen?'

'Yes, but——'

'So why not take their advice? Stop fretting at it.'

'So why don't *you* take their advice too?' she shot at him. 'Why isn't sauce for the goose sauce for the gander as well? And who are you, anyway, to tell me how to run my life?'

For a moment, as she saw the flicker of expression across his face, she thought she had gone too far. But then, to he surprise, he smiled.

'That's my Fenella,' he said lightly. 'That's the spirit.' And then he turned abruptly away, but not before she had caught the edge of another expression on his face. A minute twist of pain, of harsh regret, that she couldn't fathom. There, and gone so swiftly that she was left wondering if she had imagined it.

'So what have we decided?' he asked after a moment, as Fenella took their plates to the sideboard and came back with a bowl of fresh raspberries. 'You'll spend a few days familiarising yourself with my work—during working hours only, of course; I wouldn't expect you to spend your free time wading through it. I'll be interested to know your reactions.'

They finished their meal, talking about history and the work Robert had done up till now. To her relief, Fenella found herself relaxing now that they had left the subject of her memory loss, and able to enjoy their discussion, even countering some of Robert's remarks with views of her own. Each time this happened, she noticed that his eyes would flicker and darken as if she had said something significant, and she wondered if she offended him by her mild

disagreement. But he gave no sign that this was the
case, and she went on with a little more confidence,
feeling at the end of the meal that they had begun to
achieve a tentative rapport.

When John had come to take Robert for his
evening physiotherapy and massage, she wandered
out into the twilit garden and thought about him,
and the scent of roses wafted around her as she
wondered what it would be like to achieve a total
rapport with a man like Robert Milburn.

Presumably, she thought, someone—or maybe
more than one—had done just that in the past. He
couldn't have gone through life bereft of female
company. There must have been women—or perhaps just one woman. A woman who had been
important to him, who had caught at his affections
and held his heart. A woman who had loved him,
and whom he had loved in return.

The idea struck like a splinter in her mind and she
stopped and sank down on to a garden seat. Why
was it she had never thought of this before? Had she
been so caught up in her own personal nightmare
that she had forgotten that other people had lives
too—the syndrome that Robert had mentioned that
afternoon, thinking herself the centre of the universe? Had it really never occurred to her that
Robert would almost certainly have women
friends—that those friends might still be part of his
life, still as important as before his accident?

Indeed, why should they not?

Unwillingly, Fenella recognised the fact that
Robert, disabled as he was, was still an exceptionally
attractive man. And the fact that he had never

mentioned any woman to her meant nothing at all—
why should he give her the facts of his private life?

No doubt the woman—if woman there was—
would soon be in evidence. No doubt she would be
visiting him here, at Cowleaze. And then Fenella
would be able to see for herself.

The splinter in her mind was bigger now, and
sharper. And there was another that seemed to be
lodged firmly in her heart.

Impatiently, Fenella jumped to her feet. This she
did *not* need! To let herself be affected by the sheer
charisma of her employer, to allow his magnetism to
affect her, as if she were some impressionable teenager, was not going to help either of them.

And she was old enough to know that this was
what was threatening to happen to her. Those
strange sensations she had experienced, as if they
had met before, the odd tingle somewhere low in
her stomach when he looked at her, the ache that
spread itself through her palm and up the tender
nerves of her arm when he touched her fingers—
these were all symptoms of a physical attraction
which in other circumstances it might be fun to
enjoy. But in this situation it was a definite no-no. It
could only lead to trouble. It could not—must not—
be allowed.

There was almost certain to be a woman in Robert
Milburn's life. Fenella still did not know if there had
been a man in hers. Nor, until she regained her
memory, did she dare to admit one.

And with that thought bringing a deep sadness to
her heart, she turned and went indoors to bed.

* * *

Fenella spent the next few days doing as Robert had suggested: reading his books, exploring the house and garden, and getting to know the rest of the household—Mrs Bennett, John, and Walter, the gardener.

'We all call him that because his name's Bennett too and people might think we were married,' Mrs Bennett told Fenella as they sat on the seat outside the kitchen door one morning, drinking coffee. 'Not a mistake I'd care to encourage.'

Walter, taking his ease in a wheelbarrow, winked a bright blue eye at Fenella. 'I keep telling her we ought to tie the knot,' he said. 'Wouldn't even have to change her name.'

'No, but you'd have to change your ways,' Mrs Bennett retorted. 'Look at that shirt you're wearing today—nothing short of disgusting, that shirt is. It's all holes. I wouldn't want to take on a man who wears shirts like that.'

'But I wouldn't wear shirts like this then, would I? I mean, you wouldn't let me. You'd be mending of them, keeping me smart and tidy. You'd take a pride in it.' Walter spoke in solemn, reasonable tones but his eyes were bright and Fenella hid her smile. 'You're cut out to make some lucky man a good wife. And what I say is, why not Walter Bennett?'

'It would take too long to tell you that now, and I've got work to do if you haven't.' Mrs Bennett stood up and held out her hand. 'And, if you've finished with that mug, you can hand it over, because it's not going to get filled again this side of lunchtime. Do you like cooking?' she asked Fenella as she set the mugs back on the small tray. 'I dare say you looked after yourself in your London flat—or maybe you went out to eat most of the time; they do in London, I believe.'

Fenella smiled. Mrs Bennett had already told her that she'd been to London only twice in her life, once to something called the Festival of Britain, which had been held forty years ago, and once to go on a boat trip to Hampton Court with the local WI. Her ideas of London life seemed to have been culled from old films on TV, mostly concerning rather higher circles of society than those in which Fenella moved.

But how do I know what circles I moved in? she thought at once. And found she could not answer Mrs Bennett's question.

Fortunately, the housekeeper was already moving towards the kitchen door and didn't seem to require an answer. But Fenella's sudden check had not gone unnoticed; glancing round, she saw Walter's blue eyes fixed on her. Their twinkle had vanished and he looked unwontedly thoughtful.

Fenella looked away quickly and followed Mrs Bennett into the house. She must be more careful. She didn't want anyone else to know about her loss of memory.

She didn't want anyone thinking she was a freak.

'I told you,' Robert said, wheeling his chair to where Fenella sat in the garden, 'you don't have to read those books in your free time.'

'But I want to. This one's fascinating. And so easy to read. Almost as if——' She stopped.

'As if you'd read it before?'

'I don't know,' she said slowly. 'I suppose it's possible. I'm obviously interested in history—I must always have been. So I might well have read your books.' She looked at him, her eyes wide, grey as a troubled sea. 'But why don't I remember, like I remember *Alice* and the others?'

'Presumably because it was too recent. Anyway, don't worry about it. I'm glad you're enjoying the book now.' He paused, then asked casually, 'Don't you ever want to go out? You haven't left the garden since you came here a week ago. Why?'

'I'm quite happy here. It's a big garden.'

'But you're not seeing anyone. You're not making friends. Surely you want company?'

Fenella looked at him sharply. Something in his voice didn't quite ring true. It was as if he was simply going through the motions—saying what he thought he ought to say, while meaning something quite different. He doesn't really want me to go out at all, she thought suddenly. He just wants me to think he does. But why?

'I told you,' she said. 'I'm quite happy. I don't want—I don't feel like joining things, meeting people.' She looked at him with appeal in her eyes. 'Please don't push me, Robert.'

'Why not? I have to push myself.'

That was true, she knew. Robert was pushing himself every day, taking all the physiotherapy and massage John could give him to strengthen his muscles, working hard to develop to walk again.

'But that's different. You want to walk again. I want my memory back——'

'And I think you're wrong to strain after that. It'll either come, or it won't. You may be better off if it never does. But you ought to be trying to build your life again.'

'Why?' she asked desperately. 'Why can't I just live quietly? Robert, if I start meeting people again, I'll have to tell them. At some point, I'll have to say I can't remember anything before this spring. That's what I can't face—having to explain, over and over again, seeing that look on their faces, having to answer questions. . .' She shook her head, feeling the panic well up in her. 'I just can't.'

He looked at her for a long moment, then his hand moved to cover her quivering fingers. 'It's all right, Fenella. Don't worry. I'm not going to force you. But. . .one day, you're going to have to force yourself.'

'I know. But not until I'm ready.' She met his eyes, as grey as her own, and felt again that strange shock of recognition. . . It was nothing but physical attraction, she told herself desperately, the normal chemistry between a man and a woman thrown together in close proximity. It had to be controlled. People encountered it every day, at work, in offices, in all sorts of situations, and they disciplined themselves not to give way to it. Otherwise the fabric of civilisation would break down completely. . . And she was feeling it the more because she was particularly vulnerable at present, just as some women fell in love with their doctors.

It meant nothing. *Nothing*.

Nevertheless, she could not stay here, with his hand over hers and his eyes looking into hers with that disturbing intensity. Not without betraying the effect he was having on her. And that she could not—dared not— do.

'I'm sorry, Robert,' she said shakily. 'I have to go indoors. The sun. . .' She twisted her hand away from his and stood up, almost dropping her book, then turned and fled.

Back in her room, looking down at the sunlit garden, she scolded herself for her irrational behaviour. What had Robert done that she should run from him like that? What must he be thinking of her now?

If you're not careful, she told herself, going to the mirror and staring at the reflected face, pale under the dark hair, her eyes grey as clouds, he's going to think again about having you here to work for him. You'll have to leave—go back to London—and then you'll *really* have to start building your own life again.

The thought slid into her mind like a sliver of ice, and struck coldly at her heart. And she knew that staying here at Cowleaze, with Robert, was her lifeline. For her, leaving would be the beginning of the end.

But was it Cowleaze and the protection offered by its quiet tranquillity, the haven of its mellow walls, that she needed? Or was it Robert himself?

By the second week, Fenella had read two of Robert's books and was absorbed in a third. She wondered if she had indeed read them before. They were well-known, one of them had even reached the list of bestsellers, and she had an odd sense, not quite of familiarity, but more of reaching into the mind of their author, as she read them. As if Robert were speaking to her from the pages, telling her more than the words themselves. The sensation disturbed her and she would close the book, trembling a little, and stare across the sunlit garden as if asking a question.

But she didn't know what the question must be. And how could the garden give her an answer?

'You look very thoughtful. Shall I give you a penny for them? Or has the price risen in line with inflation?'

Fenella jumped violently and the book fell from her hands. Her heart thudding, she looked up into the face of a complete stranger—a young man with brown, curly hair and blue eyes that laughed at her and invited her to laugh back. As she stared at him, the laughter faded and was replaced by a look of concern.

'I say, I really scared you, didn't I? I'm truly sorry—don't look so terrified. I'm not going to hurt you.' He sat down beside her on the garden seat and took her unresisting hand. 'Look, can I get you anything? You've gone really pale. Honestly, I never dreamed——'

'It's all right.' Fenella raised a shaking hand to her head. 'I'll be all right in a moment. It's not your fault.' She managed a wavering smile. 'I've been ill, you see—I jump a bit, it's silly. . .'

'Not silly at all,' he said. He had a light, pleasant voice. 'I'm the fool, for startling you like that. I'm Andrew Bennett, by the way—Mrs Bennett's my

Aunt Rose. I'm staying in the village for a few weeks, so I called in to see her.'

'Mrs Bennett's your aunt?'

'Well, more like a second cousin, really, but I've always called her aunt. She's always been good to me—especially since Mum died.' A shadow crossed his face. 'So when she knew I wanted a room somewhere to stay while I do some work on my post-graduate thesis, she suggested a place in Winchcombe. Friend of hers, done bed and breakfast for years but she's getting a bit old for it now—all that bed-changing and never knowing who's coming next, you know—and she jumped at the chance of having a nice, well-brought-up young man as a long-stay lodger.' He grinned, and the laughter was back in his eyes. 'And I'm in clover—treated like a prince. Glorious countryside to walk in—have you done much walking hereabouts? In fact, I don't think I'm going to want to leave.' He stretched his arms and lifted his face to the sun. 'And Winchcombe's fascinating, don't you think?'

Fenella shook her head, slightly overwhelmed by the newcomer's exuberance. 'I don't know. I haven't been there yet.'

'Haven't been there?' He lowered his arms and looked at her in astonishment. 'But how long have you been here?'

'About. . .' She stopped to think, surprised that she had to. 'About eleven days.'

'Nearly a fortnight and you haven't even been to the town? Oh, but you said you'd been ill, didn't you.' He inspected her. 'You look quite well now—

now that you've got over the shock of seeing me, anyway! Was it anything serious?'

'An accident. I'm better now, but——'

'Well, then you'll have to let me show you round,' he declared cheerfully. 'I've only been here a couple of weeks myself, but I feel quite part of the furniture. Why not come now and have tea with me? There's a marvellous little place right in the middle of the town, and we could——'

'I thought you said you'd come to see your aunt?'

'Oh, yes, so I did. Well, I suppose I'd better do that. I wouldn't like to hurt Aunt Rose's feelings. Tomorrow, then. Come and have coffee and I'll show you the church. There are some marvellous old gargoyles around the roof, you must see those. And there's——'

'I'm not sure,' Fenella broke in. 'I mean, I'm not sure I can come. I'm not here on holiday, you see—I work here. I—I'm a research assistant and secretary.'

'Oh.' For a moment, the young face looked crestfallen. 'But you get time off, don't you? I mean, he doesn't make you work *all* the time. You are allowed out?'

'Yes, of course. It's just that up till now I—haven't wanted to.'

'But you want to now,' Andrew stated confidently. 'And there's so much to see around here. The castle, of course—did you know that one of Henry the Eighth's wives lived here? Katherine Parr, the one who actually managed to outlive the old Bluebeard. And wonderful countryside—do you like walking?'

'Yes, but——'

'Look, tell me to go if you'd rather,' he said suddenly. 'I don't want to force my company on you if it's not wanted.'

Fenella looked at him. There was no sarcasm in the words—he was simply giving her the choice. She felt suddenly ashamed of her reluctant response to his friendliness, and put out an impulsive hand.

'I'm sorry—I'm being rude. It's just that since the accident I haven't really wanted to go out much—I had a knock on the head, you see, and it's rather affected me. I mean, I've lost confidence. I know I have to make an effort to get over it, but it's not easy to start.'

'I see. Well, why not start gradually?' He gave her his own friendly smile. 'Like by having coffee with me and a nice, gentle stroll round the church. Do you work regular hours with Professor Milburn?'

She looked at him in surprise. 'You know him?'

'I know *of* him. Aunt Rose has told me a bit about him. And his name's well known.' He glanced at her curiously. 'You sound surprised.'

Fenella shook her head. 'I haven't started working regular hours yet. I'm just familiarising myself with his books.' She indicated the one on her lap.

'Then there's nothing to stop you coming out for an hour or two, is there? Especially if you haven't been outside the place for eleven days. So—shall we say coffee tomorrow morning?' He rose to his feet. 'That's unless you'd rather not?' And she looked at him to see that there was a trace of real anxiety in his face as he watched her.

Fenella hesitated, then made up her mind. She had to take the plunge some time. She had to face the world, start to interact with people once more, risk their questions and handle any that might be asked. And it might as well be with this friendly, inconsequential young man.

'I'd like to come,' she said. 'Thank you.'

Andrew's face relaxed. 'That's wonderful! Look, I'll meet you at—let's say ten-thirty, shall we? Or, no, you don't know the town at all—I'll come and call for you. It's only a short walk. And we'll have coffee together and one of their wicked cakes, and I'll show you the church. You really ought to see those gargoyles!' He grinned. 'And now I'd better go and see Aunt Rose. She'll be wondering where I've got to.'

He gave Fenella a cheerful wave and disappeared in the direction of the house.

'And who,' Robert asked, appearing round the bend in the path in his wheelchair, 'was that young man?'

Fenella jumped again, feeling almost guilty this time, as if caught doing something forbidden.

'It's Andrew—Mrs Bennett's nephew. Well, second cousin really, but he's always called her aunt. He's staying in the village doing a post-graduate thesis——' She stopped abruptly, conscious of the ironic look in Robert's steel-grey eyes.

'You seem to know a remarkable amount about him.'

'Not much,' she protested, feeling herself flush. 'Only what he told me. He's come to see his aunt— you don't have any objection, I suppose?'

Robert shrugged. 'None at all. Mrs Bennett lives here—she's entitled to have her own visitors. I just wondered why he wasn't doing just that—visiting his aunt.'

'Instead of talking to me, you mean?' Fenella felt a small ripple of anger. 'Well, he was just walking through the garden and happened to notice me on this seat as he went past. And, being a polite, friendly person, stopped to say hello and introduce himself. I wouldn't have thought there was anything to object to in that myself, but perhaps you have other ideas.'

'My dear girl, there's no need to bite my head off.' He sounded bored, his head turned slightly away from her, eyes fixed on something in the distance. 'He does seem to have done more than simply say hello, though—from what you say, he's told you half his life story. But there, it's none of my business.' He paused, then added offhandedly, 'Staying in the village, you say?'

'That's right.'

'So I suppose we'll be seeing more of him at Cowleaze? Visiting his aunt, or whatever relation Mrs Bennett is to him.'

'Yes,' Fenella said after a moment. 'I suppose we shall.'

'Hmm.' Robert said nothing for a minute or two. Then he glanced at her. 'Well, don't let him become too friendly, Fenella. Don't forget, you're still in a vulnerable state. I wouldn't like to see you get hurt.'

Get hurt! Fenella stared at him. Just what was he implying? Just what sort of girl did he imagine she was?

'Look, I spoke to Andrew Bennett for only a few minutes. He was pleasant and friendly, nothing more. What's wrong with that? I thought you *wanted* me to meet people—make friends.'

'Yes, yes, of course.' He spoke impatiently. 'But that particular young man—well, he strikes me as just the sort who might fancy a little romance to take his mind off what he's supposed to be doing. Don't forget, I've worked in universities, I've seen all this before—a bored young man, supposed to be studying and all too easily distracted by the summer weather and a pretty girl. And it's invariably the girl who gets hurt.'

'I see,' Fenella said coldly. 'Well, since I managed to reach the ripe old age of twenty-six without appearing to have got hurt in that particular way——' she paused, catching her breath: how did she *know*? '—I think we may take it that I can look after myself reasonably well in that direction. It's kind of you to be so concerned about me, but, since I must be at least a couple of years older than Andrew Bennett, I think I can cope with any "danger" he might present to me. And now, If you'll excuse me, I think I'll go in and have some tea. I imagine Mrs Bennett has made it by now—that's if she hasn't been too distracted herself by the bored young man you're so worried about.'

She stood up, turned her back and walked away from him, hoping that the thudding of her heart and the shaking of her knees were not apparent to Robert Milburn as he watched her go. Speaking to him like that had taken a real effort—but the anger that still burned somewhere inside had helped. And she couldn't allow him to speak to her like that, in that *patronising* manner.

All the same, she acknowledged that the effect he had on her was showing no sign of lessening. One word, one sword-like glance from those silvery eyes, contained more impact than all Andrew's puppylike eagerness.

It was as well that she had managed to conceal that impact. And it might, she decided, be a very good thing if Robert were to go on thinking that she could be interested in Andrew Bennett.

If she was in peril at all, it wasn't from Andrew. And she most definitely did not want Robert to guess where lay the real danger to her heart.

CHAPTER FOUR

FENELLA walked down the curving drive, between the trees, and emerged on to the road.

She had not told Robert about her arrangement with Andrew. The small flare of anger that had sustained her during her outburst in the garden yesterday had continued to burn, preventing her from mentioning Mrs Bennett's young relative again. Anyway, she told herself, it was none of Robert's business. If she chose to go and have coffee and look around the local church with Andrew at ten-thirty in the morning—heavens, what possible harm could there be in that?

And why should she feel even faintly guilty at not having told Robert?

All the same, she had decided it would be better to go out to meet Andrew rather than have him come to the house. And, although she had left in plenty of time, she wasn't a moment too soon, for here he was now, strolling along the road in the easy, loose-limbed way that she remembered from yesterday, lifting a hand in casual greeting as he saw her, his mouth widening in the friendly grin that made Robert's warning seem so ridiculous.

'Hi! Isn't it a glorious morning?' He stopped and raised his arms to the sun. 'The best summer we've had for about five years—seems a crime to stay indoors on a morning like this.'

'And I suppose that's where we both ought to be,' she remarked, falling in beside him as he turned to walk back down the hill to the town. 'You studying and me researching.'

'I studied all last evening,' he said quickly. 'What's your excuse?'

Fenella laughed. 'I'm not wanted this morning. Robert's still working on something he doesn't need my help with. Anyway, he's my employer, not my gaoler.'

They walked without speaking for a few minutes. Then he said, 'Did you really mean what you told me—that you'd not been outside the garden since you came here?'

'Yes,' she said cautiously, and thought of how she had told Robert of her fear of being asked questions. Tension began to tighten her nerves.

'Then you won't have seen anything of Winchcombe. Churches, gates, gargoyles—you name it, I can show it to you. Now, don't you think you were exceptionally lucky to fall in with me?'

'Oh, but of course. The wonder is that you haven't collected an eager crowd of tourists, all hanging on your every word and taking photographs to show the folks back home.'

'Don't think I haven't thought of it,' he said. 'There's a big market for showing people around this country. Private parties of Americans, wanting to see all the beauties of England that other couriers can't reach. We'd travel by limousine, of course——'

'But naturally. And stay in the best hotels.'

'I'd never think of anything else. Though they do

like the odd spot of bed and breakfast too, you know. Dear old souls like my Mrs Taggart, with quaint bedrooms in the roof and producing marvellous breakfasts with home-made marmalade. Yes, I reckon I could build up a good business if I put my mind to it.'

They had passed the castle gates now and arrived by a row of picturesque cottages, their ancient stone façades draped with the gnarled branches and drooping mauve flowers of wistaria. Opposite the church walls, Andrew turned right and led Fenella into a small cake shop with a tea-room behind it.

'Let's sit out in the garden. We've already agreed it's too nice to be indoors.'

'Would you put your mind to it, Andrew?' Fenella asked when the waitress had taken their order.

He looked startled for a moment, then grinned. 'You mean the courier business? No, I don't think so. I prefer one-to-one guided tours.' He gave her a quick glance. 'Much pleasanter.'

Fenella smiled at him. 'So just what do you put your mind to?'

'Sorry?'

'You told me you were working on a post-graduate thesis. So presumably you do work sometimes.'

'Oh, that! Very boring, I'm afraid. Not the sort of thing I like to talk about in mixed company, especially on a beautiful morning like this. Ah— here's our coffee and scones. I say, they look good.' He grinned at the waitress. 'You've surpassed yourself this morning, Sarah. Sarah does a lot of the cooking here,' he added to Fenella, 'which is why I can so often be found stuffing myself with scones and millionaires' shortbread when I ought to be working. You'll make some lucky man a wonderful wife some day,' he told the girl, who blushed scarlet and hurried away.

'You've embarrassed her,' Fenella told him, but he shook his head.

'Sarah and I understand each other. Now, how do you like your coffee? Black, white or navy blue?'

They strolled round the little town, then went over to the church and wandered around the outside. 'Come and look at these.' He led her to the side of the church and pointed upwards. 'Aren't they marvellous?'

Fenella looked up and laughed. The gargoyles were like characters from some Disney cartoon, their faces grim, ugly or comical, and they stared down as they had stared for centuries in an attempt to intimidate unworthy churchgoers.

'I've heard they're supposed to be local dignitaries who'd annoyed the church masons,' Andrew said. 'If so, the masons certainly got their revenge! Look at that one—he looks as if he'd got a particularly painful toothache.'

'They're wonderful,' Fenella agreed, then glanced at her watch and gave an exclamation of surprise.

'Heavens, look at the time! I'd no idea it was so late. I'll have to go back now—Robert will be wondering where I am.'

'Oh, you don't really have to go, do you? I was hoping you'd have lunch with me.' He looked appealingly at her, but Fenella shook her head.

'I'm sorry, Andrew, but I didn't tell anyone I was going out, and if I'm not there for lunch they'll worry. Another day, perhaps—I've really enjoyed this morning.' She was already walking quickly back towards the road which led past the castle.

'Tomorrow, then?'

Fenella hesitated. 'I'd like to come out with you again, Andrew, I really would. But I can't make any arrangements now. Why don't you give me a ring? And now I really will have to hurry.'

'All right, then.' He walked back with her to the gates of Cowleaze. 'I suppose I'd better let you go now. But I shan't forget to ring. I'm going to hold you to that promise of a walk, with a pub lunch somewhere.'

'I'm looking forward to it already. I'm sure I'll be able to arrange a day soon. Robert won't mind a bit—why should he?'

Why, indeed? she thought as she walked up the drive. There was no reason at all. But she had an uneasy feeling that he would, all the same.

'Where on earth have you been?' Robert greeted her as she appeared on the terrace where they took meals on fine days. 'John and Mrs Bennett have been looking for you everywhere. We thought something had happened to you.'

'Like what? Being spirited away by the fairies for seven years?' Irritated, Fenella took one of the white chairs and poured herself some iced mineral water. 'I'm sorry I'm late, but I understood lunch was only a snack affair anyway. You're not always on time yourself. And there was no need to worry about me.'

'We didn't know that, did we?' he retorted. 'There

might have been every need. You've been making it
clear enough that you were too scared to go outside
the gates, so what are we supposed to think when
you disappear for a whole morning on your
own? I——'

'I wasn't on my own!' Fenella snapped, and then
bit her lip. There was no reason at all why she
shouldn't have told him she'd been with Andrew—
but, all the same, she hadn't meant to. She took a
piece of French bread and spread it with soft,
melting Brie before adding as coolly as she could
manage, 'I was with a friend.'

'A friend?' Dark brows snapped down over glinting grey eyes. 'I understood you didn't know anyone
around here.'

'I didn't. Now, I do. I was with Andrew Bennett—
Mrs Bennett's nephew. And, if you want to know
what we did, we had coffee together and then looked
at the church.' She lifted her head and met his eyes
with a direct, challenging glance. 'Is that innocent
enough for you?'

Robert looked exasperated. 'Fenella, you don't
have to explain yourself to me——'

'Oh? I was under the impression that was just
exactly what I did have to do.'

'Don't be ridiculous! All I want is——'

'—To know just where I am and what I'm doing
at every moment of every day,' Fenella declared
furiously. 'That's *all* you want, isn't it? To keep me
in some kind of cage. Well, I won't be caged! I won't
be treated like some kind of freak who mustn't be
let out alone. If I'm to go on working here for you,

Professor Milburn, I must have my own free
time——'

'Fenella, you do have your own free time——'

'And it must *be* my time,' she went on, thrusting
past his interruption. 'Mine to do as I like with—
and not to have to explain.' She stopped and looked
at him, aware suddenly of her raised voice, of its
carrying quality in the open air. They must be able
to hear her down in the village! Lowering her tone,
she said more reasonably, 'If I were working in your
office, you wouldn't be worrying about where I was
during my free time, or who I was with.'

There was a moment's silence. Robert looked at
her, and she caught a tiny but distinct change in his
expression, as if there was something he wanted to
say in reply. His eyes flickered. Then he said, quietly
and equably, as if there were nothing else in his
mind at all, 'No, perhaps I wouldn't. But that would
be different, wouldn't it? You're living in my house.
I feel some measure of responsibility for you, particularly knowing your. . .difficulty. Is that so
unreasonable? Especially as you haven't been in the
habit of going out until now.'

Fenella met his eyes and felt ashamed. 'No,' she
said reluctantly. 'No, it isn't unreasonable. You're
quite right. I should have let you know.'

His eyes held hers and again she had the strange
feeling that he was trying to tell her something,
trying to say more than his words could convey. For
a brief instant, too, she felt that odd familiarity she
had sensed before—as if she already knew him, as if
he had never been a stranger. Her skin tingled. She
looked down and saw his hand on the table, the

fingers close to hers, almost close enough to touch, and the sense increased. Yet how could it be anything other than an illusion? How could they ever have known each other in that other, forgotten life?

She gazed across the garden, and felt a bleak desolation that struck to the core of her heart. And knew in that moment that she would have given anything to have known Robert Milburn in that strange limbo from which she had come. For if she had known him, she must have known security— and love.

It was too late now for her and Robert. But at another time, in another life, it would have been right. And the pain of what might have been, the loss of something she had never known and now never would, filled her heart with tears.

With no more than a mumble of apology, she stood up and ran for the house, leaving Robert on the terrace, in the wheelchair that was his cage as surely as her lost memory was hers.

It was during that week that Robert decided he should begin work in earnest, and Fenella found herself kept busy during the days, working with him on the new book, looking up references and researching in the extensive library that occupied one room of the house. She was soon engrossed in the work and found little time to think of Andrew or their tentative plans to go for a long walk together. And in the evenings, when Robert declared work over for the day, she was either too exhausted to think of going out or too interested in what they had been doing, ready to continue discussing it over dinner and late into the evening.

'People must have suffered dreadfully in sieges,' she said thoughtfully as they ate one of Mrs Bennett's beautifully cooked meals. 'Imagine having to eat your own pets! And, even worse, catching rats.' She shuddered. 'I'd much rather have this delicious poached salmon—it's my favourite.'

There was a sudden tiny silence. Fenella looked at her plate, at the few scraps of deep pink fish still on it. How had she known that? Yet it was true, she was sure—she had always loved poached salmon. She looked up to find Robert's eyes on her.

'You know that, don't you?' he said, echoing her thoughts. 'You knew it even before you began to eat.' He leaned forward and his voice shook suddenly with some deep emotion. 'How did you know, Fenella? Do you remember eating it before—in some special place, perhaps? With. . .some special person?'

Fenella stared at him. His eyes had darkened to deep charcoal, his nostrils were tensely flared, the muscles of his cheeks taut. She could feel the tension in him, touching her own nerves with an urgency that set them quivering. She caught her breath. He *knew*. He knew what she had been thinking. But how. . .? Why. . .?

How could this man, whom she could never have known before, understand so well what was in her heart?

She dropped her glance before the intensity in his eyes compelled her to speak. In that moment, she knew that she dared not trust her voice; it was liable to say all kinds of things she didn't even know were in her mind.

'They even ate the zoo animals during the Siege of Paris,' she whispered at last. 'That poor old elephant. . .' Her voice faded away into silence, and she dared not look up.

To her relief, Robert followed up her remark; perhaps he too had been disconcerted by the sudden tension between them.

'It wasn't only during that siege that people were so desperate,' he said. 'The same thing would have happened in any of them, once food began to run out. It's surprising how unsqueamish human beings can be when they're really hungry. . . Something we could learn from. Total deprivation brings in a whole new code of behaviour.'

'And a lot of ingenuity, too,' Fenella added, feeling as if she were talking on auto-pilot, following a script that had been written a long time ago. 'Those articles I've been reading today—about how they made balloons with fabrics like taffeta from Paris fashion houses, and flew out pigeons which would be sent back with instructions from the military headquarters outside Paris—it's amazing how quickly they had it all arranged and operating. And how even ordinary people could use the balloon as a post office and send letters out to their friends.' She stopped. Why was she talking like this? Was it because she was afraid to stop—afraid of the words that might fill the silence if they allowed it develop? What was happening?

And did Robert really feel it too—or was she imagining the tautness in his voice, the impression that under his words was a message of quite a different sort?

'*And* paid for special stamps,' he said. 'You can rely on the French for seeing the commercial possibilities of their own ingenuity. And why not? The balloons had to be paid for.'

He paused and at once the tension gathered, like shadows encroaching from the corner of the room.

Fenella lifted her head and stared at him. His eyes were on hers, dark and smouldering. His hands were on the table, close to hers. She could feel the tiny hairs touching her skin, quivering slightly. A tingle ran through her skin, deepening to a slow ache, and her heart began to hammer against her ribs.

'I. . .' She began, and found she'd forgotten what she meant to say. She took a deep breath and moved her hands away, then stood up. She felt as stiff as if she had been sitting there for a very long time. 'I'll take the things out to the kitchen. . .'

Without looking at Robert again, she gathered up their empty plates and carried them out of the room. As soon as the door was closed behind her, she leaned against the wall, waiting for her heart to slow its frantic beating, waiting for her breath to return to normal. What on *earth* was the matter with her? What had been happening in there?

It was, she thought, as if she and Robert had been re-enacting a scene, a conversation, that had all happened before. Even the food they had been eating, the articles they had been discussing—all had a strange familiarity. Yet it was—it *must* be— impossible.

Déjà vu, she thought. Even people who haven't

lost their memories experience it. It has no more significance than that.

Yet how could she tell?

With an effort, she moved down the passage towards the kitchen. What she needed now was normality—the cheerful, matter-of-fact presence and conversation of Mrs Bennett. She opened the kitchen door and went in.

To her surprise, Andrew was there, eating at the kitchen table. He looked up and grinned as Fenella came in, and waved a spoon at her.

'Hello, stranger. Come to see how the other half lives?'

Fenella took a breath, but couldn't help feeling pleased to see him. Hadn't she wanted normality, after all? And there could be no one more engagingly normal than Andrew. She set the plates down by the sink and gave Mrs Bennett a smile.

'That was delicious. I spent most of the meal feeling sorry for people who don't get to eat your meals.'

'Like me,' Andrew said mournfully. 'While the upstairs folk are tucking into lobster thermidor, what do I get? Tinned soup and a crust of bread.'

'Don't be sillier than you can help,' his aunt said sharply. 'That soup's never seen a tin, as well you know. Now, Miss Fenella, there's raspberry pancakes to follow, and cheese as usual. Can you manage the tray?'

'Or shall I be waiter?' Andrew enquired. 'I worked in quite a high-class restaurant once. I can carry plates all up my arm. I'll show you——'

'Don't you dare! Miss Fenella can manage perfectly well without your help. Now, you just sit down and finish that soup and I'll scramble you some eggs. Don't you take any notice of him,' Mrs Bennett said to Fenella. 'He's always been too full of cheek for his own good, this one.' But the look she gave him was affectionate, and Fenella smiled as she lifted the tray.

'Hey, don't go yet!' Andrew exclaimed as she turned to the door. 'I came specially to see you. Where have you been this past week? I thought we were going to go for a long walk.'

'I'm sorry, I've been busy.' And had almost forgotten their half-made arrangement, she thought in surprise. 'But I should think I could have a day off at the weekend—perhaps we could go tomorrow if the weather's fine?'

'It will be,' Andrew declared positively. 'I'll arrange it myself. Morning? Afternoon?' His brows rose as Fenella hesitated. 'Heavens, girl, you must have *some* idea when you'll have time off! What sort of a slave-driver is this professor?'

'He's not a slave-driver at all,' Fenella defended him. 'All right—morning. I'll meet you at the gate at——'

'Ten-thirty,' Andrew said as she paused again. 'And, if you're late, I'll come up and drag you away by force. You've been warned!'

'Ten-thirty,' Fenella agreed. 'And now I must go back—he'll be wondering where I've got to with the dessert. Thanks, Mrs Bennett—the pancakes look delicious.' She gave Andrew a mischievous glance. 'We may even leave you a scrap. Enjoy your scrambled eggs!'

Going back to the dining-room, she felt oddly light-hearted and wondered where the mood of a few minutes ago had gone, and whether the tension would still be there when she returned to Robert. She hesitated at the door, her nerves tightened slightly, then went in. But there was still a small smile on her face, and Robert gave her a sharp glance as she came in.

'You look as if you've been having a good time out there. Mrs Bennett putting on a floor show?'

'No, of course not,' Fenella said, laughing at a sudden vision of the stout cook in feathers, doing a high-kicking dance on the kitchen table. 'Her nephew's there—Andrew. We've just arranged to go for a walk tomorrow.'

'A walk!' He stared at her. 'What kind of a walk?'

'Well, the usual kind, I suppose. You know, on our feet.' She stopped abruptly and bit her lip. 'I'm sorry—I wasn't thinking.' Feeling her face colour painfully, she slid two raspberry pancakes on to his plate.

'Yes, I imagined that was the kind you meant,' he said quietly. 'The sort I can't go for any more.' He raised his head and looked at her, his eyes bright as steel. 'But I shall, Fenella, I shall.'

She looked at him and felt a sudden pang of remorse and compassion. How selfish I've become, she thought. Thinking only of myself and my own problems, and giving no thought at all to his. Yet it was his courage and determination that had first drawn her to him. She remembered that first glimpse of him, swooping down the field in his wheelchair in pursuit of a ball—an activity that might have seemed trivial to any man with the full use of his legs, yet which had taken on a deadly importance in Robert Milburn's eyes.

'I know you will,' she said, and leant forward to lay her hand impulsively over his. 'You can't fail to. You'll walk again, I know it—yes, and do all the other things you love to do too. Climb—ski—swim—all of them.'

'All of them,' he repeated slowly, his eyes on the fingers she had unthinkingly curled around his. 'I wonder. . .will I? Will I do all the things I love to do, Fenella? The things I did before?' He lifted his head suddenly and his glance met hers like a blow, the twin swords lancing into her mind as if to read her most secret thoughts, so secret that even she was unaware of them. 'Will I?' he repeated, and the intensity in his voice as it throbbed low between them brought back all the sensations she had experienced earlier—as if there were something here she ought to know, some emotion that should be recognised and acknowledged.

For a heartbeat of time, she left her hand in his and let her nerves receive his message, let them answer it with her own. And then, inexplicably afraid, she drew her fingers away.

Immediately, the spell was broken. Robert moved abruptly, his face closed, eyes veiled. He picked up his fork.

'I'm sorry. I'm letting self-pity get the better of me. So you're going out with young Bennett tomorrow, are you?'

For a moment, Fenella had to struggle to remember what they had been talking about. Then she nodded, though the thought of a walk with Andrew had somehow lost its allure. She knew suddenly that she would rather be spending the day here with Robert, even in his surliest mood, than out with Andrew at his most flippant.

'Yes,' she said drearily. 'That's if you've no objection.'

He gave her a quick, almost dismissive glance and she saw with a pang how drawn his face was, how tired he looked. What had happened to their rapport? she thought sadly. Such moments seemed doomed to come only in brief flashes, too fragile to survive. Yet the feeling was still strong within her that there ought to be some kind of deeper understanding between them—if only she could grasp the thread that was so maddeningly, tormentingly elusive. . .

'No,' Robert said in a tired voice, and she wrenched her mind back to her own last words. 'No, I've no objection. How could I have? You go out with Andrew Bennett if you want to, and have a good long walk.' He pushed his plate aside. 'I can't eat any more of this—tell Mrs Bennett it was delicious, but I over-ate on the first course. And I think I'll forgo coffee this evening—I'll just get John to put me to bed.'

There was a bleakness in his voice as he said those last words, and Fenella felt once again the bitterness of an active man trapped in a wheelchair, doomed perhaps to spend the rest of his life there. Unable to go for walks, to fetch himself a book, even to go to bed without help. . . It was no wonder that he was irascible at times, that he was jealous of a young, healthy man like Andrew who could come and go as he pleased. No wonder that he should take out his frustration on the nearest person—who happened to be Fenella.

There was nothing personal in it, she told herself as she called John and wished her employer goodnight. It was nothing to do with her at all. In fact, she doubted whether he even saw her as a person most of the time. She was, after all, no more than an employee—a secretary and researcher. And when he had finished his present book, and was once more walking, as he was so determined to do, he would have no further use for her.

She would have to look for another job then. And make yet another new start at building her life.

With a sense of desolation, Fenella realised that this new attempt would be far harder than the first. She had leaned on Robert more than she had known. To lose his support would leave her truly alone.

And not simply alone, she thought with a bleak sense of what she might be losing. More than that.

Bereft.

'And I think that's enough for today. I've worked you quite hard enough.'

Robert spoke impersonally, as he had been doing all day, and Fenella gathered her papers together with a tiny sigh. Ever since Saturday evening, he had been treating her with this cool detachment, as if she were no more than an employee—— She caught herself up sharply. She *was* no more than an employee, after all. . . But she couldn't help remembering those few brief moments when they had seemed to share something more, some unspoken intimacy. And, as she recalled them, she felt a cold loneliness around her heart.

She hadn't seen Robert before going out to meet Andrew the previous morning and the thought of him had been in her mind all day, even as she strolled through the fields with her mind only half on the jokes and laughter that were so much a part of Andrew's personality. Had he really shared those moments, or was it just a part of her own heated imagination? And what was happening to her, that she felt so intensely when she was with him—and only half alive when she was not?

When she'd arrived back, after a long day in the open air, she felt almost afraid to meet him again, trembling at the thought of meeting those silver-grey eyes, sharing an evening alone. . . But Robert had been nowhere to be seen when Andrew brought her back, and when she'd come down to dinner after a bath it was to find that he'd decided to eat alone in his room and go to bed early. She'd felt both deflated and relieved. And the evening had seemed endless.

Now, at the end of a day's work, she felt as if she had been firmly relegated to the position of employee, with no hint that there might have been any chance of any closer relationship between them. All day, Robert had treated her with the same chilly politeness. All day, she had felt her misery growing, like a hard, immovable lump in her breast. And there was nothing she could say, nothing she could do.

'I really don't mind working a little longer,' she offered. 'It's not five yet.'

'I said that would be enough.' There was a tight irritation in his voice. 'Put your papers away, Fenella. I've had enough, even if you haven't.'

Subdued, she began to pack away her typewriter. Robert wheeled himself over to the french window, which stood open, and stared moodily out over the garden and the wooded hills beyond.

Fenella watched him for a moment, knowing that he could not see her. Her heart ached with sudden emotion, and she took a small, involuntary step towards him. In that second, she knew just what was the matter with her—just what the emotion was that filled her heart with yearning. She knew why she had felt bereft at the thought of leaving him, why she had not enjoyed her day out with Andrew, why Robert Milburn had become so important to her, the focus of her world.

Her lips parted and, soundlessly, shaped his name. And, as they did so, he spun his chair round and saw her.

There was a moment of brief, electric silence.

'*Fenella . . .*' he breathed, and raised himself in the chair.

It was never quite possible, afterwards, to remember just what happened next.

Fenella's most vivid memory was of the expression on Robert's face as he stared at her; then the dawning astonishment in his eyes as he realised that he was almost on his feet; then her own cry as she ran forward and caught him in her arms so that they half crouched, swaying together, at the edge of the seat before he fell back into it, breathing hard, laughing and groaning all at once. And her terror that he might have done himself irreparable harm.

'We must call the doctor straight away,' she said, kneeling beside him, her hands over his wrist as she tried to count his wildly pounding pulse. 'Sam—I'll ring Sam. He'll still be at the hospital. Or should I call the local——?'

'There's no need to call anyone.' His face was alight. 'Don't you realise, Fenella—I almost stood up then? *I almost stood up*. That means I'm getting better. You don't call doctors when you're getting *better*, for heaven's sake.'

'You do in these circumstances,' she said firmly and got to her feet. 'I'm going to ring Sam this minute. You stay there.' As she spoke the words, she thought with a leap of her heart that a few minutes ago they would have been ridiculous, even cruel. 'Don't even *think* about trying to do it again.' She went out to the hall to telephone, forgetting the instrument that stood on Robert's desk. In any case, she would hardly have been able to speak to Sam with Robert sitting there, gazing at her with that almost luminous expression on his face.

As she sat on the chair and waited for Sam to be paged, she took several deep breaths, to steady her own frantic heartbeat, and thought again over those few incredible moments.

What had caused Robert to lift himself like that? Was it really because he had turned and seen the expression on her own face? Had he seen, as he seemed so often to see, what was dawning in her heart? Had he tuned in to her feelings, so powerfully that even his disability could not keep him from coming to her?

She shook her head. It was impossible. She mustn't even think that way. She must forget the look on his face as he'd turned, forget the emotion in her own heart that had betrayed her to him. It could only complicate things—and their lives were quite complicated enough already.

So she loved Robert Milburn. And that was why she had those flashes of familiarity—a sensation known to lovers through the ages, that they must at some time, in another age, another life, have met and loved before. But that was where it ended. Robert felt nothing for her, other than a compassion for her own disability. Nothing.

She must forget that look. Forget the way she had run across the room towards him. Forget the way she'd held him close and felt his arms strong and hard around her, for those few brief seconds before he had fallen back into his wheelchair.

Forget the way she had kissed him then; and the way he had kissed her.

It meant nothing. Only a momentary shared excitement. No more than that—to Robert Milburn.

A sudden crackle from the telephone brought her back sharply to the present and she gathered her thoughts and spoke into it.

'Sam? Is that you? It's Fenella here. I've got some news for you. . .'

CHAPTER FIVE

'AMAZING,' Sam said as he and Robert came into the dining-room. 'Quite amazing.'

'You believe me, then?' Robert said, and turned to Fenella and John, grinning triumphantly. 'He believes me!'

'Oh, that's wonderful,' Fenella said, smiling back, and John added,

'Congratulations. Now I suppose I'll have to start looking for another job.'

'Not so fast,' Sam said, sitting down at the table and tucking his napkin under his chin. 'All we've ascertained is that there's some feeling in the legs—it may never come to any more than that. And Robert must see his own consultant—don't forget, this isn't really my field. Though I think he'll say the same thing. . . You're not going to leap up and start skiing again,' he told Robert. 'Not immediately, and perhaps never. Don't raise any false hopes.'

'I'm not *hoping* for anything.' Robert's face was grim as he manoeuvred his chair into position. 'I'm determined—I *will* walk again. And ski. And everything else worth while.' He glanced across the table and his eyes met and held Fenella's in a steel-bright gaze. 'Don't make any mistake, Sam. This is just the beginning.'

Fenella looked at him and felt a tremor down her spine. There was a set to his mouth, a firmness in his jaw, that told her he meant every word. If the power of the mind meant anything at all, Robert Milburn would be on his feet and doing everything he'd done before his accident, in spite of the doctors rather than because of them.

But there was more than that to his words. The look in his eyes was purely for her—as if that future was to be equally important to her. And the thought was so daunting that she couldn't repress a sudden shiver.

'Whatever's happening, it'll be slow,' Sam said now. 'You've still got to be patient, Robert—and no trying to do more than you can, or you'll undo all the good that's being done. I don't want to hear about you trying to stand up or walk before you're ready, all right?'

'No, Doctor,' Robert said meekly, and Sam threw him a sharp glance. 'Scouts' honour.'

'I don't believe you ever were a Scout,' Sam said suspiciously.

'I was! I was leader of the Beaver Patrol. And I was a Wolf Cub—dib-dib-dib.' Robert was more elated and light-hearted than Fenella had ever known him. 'We had the most marvellous Akela, blonde, blue-eyed and about twenty-six——'

'Yes, well, I don't think we need to go into your misspent youth,' Sam said as Mrs Bennett brought in the first course. 'Let's concentrate on something really important. That looks absolutely delicious, Mrs Bennett. You know, the only reason I come here is to enjoy your cooking. The company's certainly nothing to write home about—with the exception of Fenella's, of course.' His face creased into even more wrinkles as he smiled across the table. 'Beats me how she stands being stuck here with you, Robert.'

'Oh, Fenella's settled down very well,' Robert said, as if she were a new kitten. 'Even has a boyfriend in the village, haven't you, Fenella? Mrs Bennett's nephew.'

There was a slight edge to his voice and Fenella felt her cheeks colour and looked down at her plate. She had been out with Andrew several times now, walking or going to the local folk dance club, and although Robert had never tried to prevent her she was aware that he disapproved of her friendship with the young student. Though what business it was of his she failed to understand. And the knowledge of his disapproval added to her determination to go out with Andrew when and where she chose.

She had even told Andrew, during that first long walk, about her lost memory, and had been comforted and reassured by his reaction.

'That doesn't make you a freak,' he said as she stumbled through her confession. 'It's nothing to be ashamed of.' He'd stopped on the footpath they were walking along, and looked at her with a serious expression she'd not seen before. 'I can understand it must be pretty awful,' he said gently. 'But it would have been worse if you'd been older. Imagine having lost forty or fifty years of your life—or even more. This way, you've still got time for a whole new life ahead of you.'

Felicity stared at him. 'I suppose I have.' She smiled suddenly. 'Thank you, Andrew. I'd never thought of it that way before.'

And when, later, Robert had made one of his edged remarks, she'd remembered that conversation and defended the younger man with some spirit.

'He's good for me,' she said. 'He makes me feel normal—as if having lost my memory isn't any big deal after all.'

'And I don't?' Robert looked at her, unsmiling. 'I make you feel like a freak?' There was a note in his voice that sounded almost like pain, and Fenella looked at him doubtfully.

'No, of course you don't. It's just that—well, Andrew's the first person outside of the hospital who's known about me. And he doesn't make a big thing of it—he doesn't ask me questions or try to make me remember. He just relaxes, and so do I.'

'I'm sorry,' Robert said stiffly, 'that you feel it so difficult to relax with me.' And before Fenella could protest or reassure him—reassure him? Could Robert really need her reassurance?—he had turned his wheelchair and propelled himself swiftly away.

Now, having made his remark to Sam, he turned the subject quickly into another channel, asking what views Sam had on the latest proposals for National Health hospitals. This was a subject on which Sam had strong opinions and they were soon deep in a discussion which involved all of them and took them through the main course and halfway into the fresh fruit salad which Fenella had helped Mrs Bennett prepare that afternoon.

'So what do you plan to do with the weekend?' Robert asked at last. 'Perhaps Fenella will take you for a walk—she must know the countryside pretty well by now.' The edge was back in his voice.

'Though I suppose you're already spoken for,' he added to Fenella. 'There don't seem to be many Sundays when you're at home.'

'Good thing too,' Sam said heartily. 'She needs a bit of company—can't expect her to spend all her time at your beck and call, Robert. I know you academics—you think nothing of burning the midnight oil and expect everyone else to do it too. You're not to work Fenella too hard, mind—I wouldn't have brought the two of you together if I'd thought you'd do that.'

Robert turned his eyes on the monkey-faced doctor for a moment and Fenella caught an odd expression in the brooding face. It was as if the two of them shared some secret. . .but then the impression was gone. Mrs Bennett came in with the coffee and Fenella got up quickly to help her clear away the plates.

'As it happens,' she said, 'Andrew's gone home this weekend. So, if Sam wants some exercise, I'd be delighted to go for a walk. Or perhaps we could go to Bourton-on-the-Water, or Snowshill, or Broadway. There's plenty to see, after all.'

'Yes,' Robert said, 'there is. Plenty.' And she caught his eyes on her again, veiled and sombre. Almost, she thought, regretful.

Yet what—apart from the obvious—did Robert Milburn have to regret?

For the first few days after Sam's visit Robert talked eagerly about the possibility—the definite promise, as he saw it—of his complete recovery. He urged

John to step up the hours of massage and physio-therapy until John protested that not only was Robert wearing himself out, he was exhausting John too. 'It won't do you any good, trying to rush things,' he said. 'You know what the doctor said—let it take its own course. It might all come to nothing.'

'It's damned well not going to!' Robert growled, but as the days went by it seemed that the brief return of sensation had been only transitory. Try as he might, he could not lift himself from the wheel-chair as he had done that first time, and his legs seemed as dead as ever.

'Can't I help at all?' Fenella asked. 'John could teach me to massage you. Or I could help with your exercises.' But Robert's face darkened and he shook his head so violently that she flinched.

'And have you see me as the useless hulk I am?' he demanded savagely. 'For pity's sake, Fenella, don't you think it's humiliating enough to be stuck here, without turning myself into an exhibition? Or do you get some perverse sort of pleasure from seeing how helpless I am?' He wheeled himself rapidly across the room and she knew that if he had been mobile he would have been striding away from her, his long legs taking him to range wide and free over the hills that lay so tantalisingly on his doorstep.

She bit her lip. Robert's fury distressed her, bringing an ache to her heart, for she knew that the bitter frustration he felt was natural to any man in his position, and perhaps even more so to Robert, so active before his accident. And he still, she thought suddenly, had never actually told her what that accident was. And the brief return of feeling, now apparently gone again, had sharpened the frustration.

His disappointment showed itself in an increasingly bad temper and Fenella, doing her best to be understanding, found his demands on her becoming almost unbearable.

'If I'm never going to be anything but a bloody cripple, again,' he snarled as they worked late into the night, 'at least I'll make my mark as a historian. It seems that's all that's left to me.'

'I'm sure it isn't,' she protested. 'You know Sam said it would take time. You just have to be patient.'

'Patient!' he exclaimed. 'While my life slips past outside the window—while other people do all the things I want to do—while you can just go swinging off over the hills with that boy Andrew Bennett, only just out of his pram—how in hell do you expect me to be *patient*, for heaven's sake?' He thrust his palms against the wheels of his chair and sent it surging across the room. 'Good lord, if you had any idea——'

'Please,' Fenella begged, 'I do try to understand— we all do. But——'

'But I'm too sorry for myself to need any more sympathy from you, is that it?' he demanded grimly. 'Well, maybe you're right. Maybe I'm turning into a selfish and querulous old man. Maybe you'd be better off finding yourself some other job, with someone who doesn't have the hang-ups I have.'

Fenella stared at him. 'But I'm happy here. I've never even thought of leaving.'

Her own words startled her. Happy? Was that really the right description of the tumult of feelings

she experienced every day in this house? The lift of
her heart as she saw Robert for the first time each
morning—so often and so abruptly crushed as his
temper grew worse and his own pain more apparent.
The way her thoughts turned to him constantly
whenever they were not together. The ache in her
body at night, as she lay sleepless in the beautiful
bedroom he had given her, with the moonlight
pouring in at the window. . .

Did all these add up to happiness? If happiness
was pain, the answer must be yes. But she knew that
leaving this house—leaving Robert—must bring an
even sharper pain.

And with that thought came the other that
haunted her mind. What of Robert's other relationships—for he must, surely, have had others?
Women he had loved—and who had loved him?
Was there one now, a special someone who waited
for him to recover from his injuries? Too far away,
perhaps, to visit him—or maybe forbidden to see
him until he was whole again. There had been
letters. . .she remembered more than one bearing
Swiss stamps, letters Robert had glanced at without
comment and then put away to read later. Were
these letters from a woman?

'I've never thought of leaving,' she repeated in a
low voice, and he turned dark grey eyes on her.

'Not while you've got a nice boyfriend in the
offing, no,' he agreed bitterly. 'But what happens
when he goes—hmm? Will you be quite so keen to
stay here once he's finished his thesis and left? It
won't be long now, will it? Has he got any idea
where he's going to go?'

Fenella felt the tears sting her eyes. Robert was increasingly like this now, bad-tempered, taunting her, as if he found relief in making her unhappy. And then, just as quickly, his mood would change and he would be remorseful and gentle, so that she knew she could never leave him. . .never. . .

'He's going to London,' she muttered. 'He's got a job lined up in——'

'All right—I'm not really interested.' Robert hesitated for a moment, then added casually, 'I suppose he's asked you to go with him?'

Fenella felt a surge of anger. 'I don't think that's any of your business.'

'No? I'd have to look for a new secretary though, wouldn't I? Well, whether he has yet or not, I'm sure he will. I would, in his shoes.' He turned away abruptly, as if sorry he had said that. 'And I suggest that if—*when*—he does, you accept. Far better than hanging on here with me. Secretaries aren't that hard to find, anyway.'

Fenella stared at him in bewilderment. 'Are you telling me you want me to go?'

'I'm telling you that I want you to do whatever you really want to do,' he said tersely. 'And I'm also telling you what I think would be best for you. And that's not being stuck in the country with a bad-tempered professor several years older than you who looks like being immobile for the rest of his life.' He turned his chair again and brought it in unnervingly close to her. 'Do you understand me?'

'I—I don't know,' Fenella stammered. She was sitting in a low chair, her face on a slightly lower level than his. She looked up into his eyes and thought suddenly what it must have been like when he could stand upright—to be close to him then, drawn into his strong arms, her face against that powerful chest.

Robert looked at her for a long moment. Then he reached out and touched her cheek with the tip of one forefinger. He drew a faint line down to her jawline, rested his knuckles gently against her neck. She quivered, feeling the tingle of his light touch spread down into her breasts. His eyes were holding hers and she saw the darkness in them and felt a twist of emotion deep in her stomach. Her lips were dry and she touched them with the tip of her tongue and saw his eyes follow the movement.

'Fenella,' he said quietly, and leaned towards her. His fingers tightened on her neck, splaying out behind her head to hold her steady, and she put out her hands and found that they came to rest almost as if it were natural against his shoulders. Almost without knowing it, she moved closer to him; she lifted her face towards him and her lips parted. She caught the darkness of his eyes, their silver colour no more than a bright rim now around the black pupil, and her stomach twisted again. She took in a tiny gasp of breath and felt a surge of panic.

But it was too late to draw back. Robert's face was close to hers, his lips brushing her mouth, and she closed her eyes as a wave of feeling broke over her. Her fingers tightened on his shoulders as his mouth fitted itself against hers, opening her lips, shaping them to his own. Gently, persuasively, his tongue touched her lips and then her teeth, finally finding its mate deep within the moistness of her mouth. Fenella moaned a little, very softly. Her arms crept up around his neck, her fingers tangling in his hair. And as she did so, she froze.

Robert drew the kiss to a close and then looked at her.

'What is it?'

'I don't know,' she whispered. 'Such an odd feeling—I can't describe it. As if—as if. . .' She shook her head. 'It's no good, It's gone.' She looked at him with uncertain eyes. 'I—I'm sorry.'

'No,' he said quietly. '*I'm* sorry. I shouldn't have done that, Fenella.' He pushed her gently away and then moved his wheelchair away. His face was bleak. 'I was right the first time,' he said bitterly. 'You'd be better off with your young, able-bodied graduate. There's nothing here for you—nothing at all.'

Fenella stared at him. She could feel the pain in her heart, spreading to her breasts as desire had done only a few moments ago. 'Robert——'

'Don't say anything more,' he said harshly. 'Don't say anything at all. The more we say, the more there is to regret.'

'Regret? But why——?'

'Why should we regret anything?' His eyes were splintered steel. 'Fenella, don't be more naïve than you can help. Look at me! Helpless, trapped in this contraption. . . What sort of a man does that make me? The sort to batten on a young, healthy woman with all the world before her?' With a quick, fierce movement of his hands, he sent the wheelchair out of her reach. 'Do you really think I've sunk that low? Well, maybe I have—maybe I would do just that, if you stayed around me much longer.' He

turned his head towards her again and now his eyes
were shadowed, pools of torment. 'Leave me a little
self-respect,' he said raggedly. 'At least let me know
that I never did that.'

Fenella lifted one hand and let it drop. She had
seen glimpses of his bitterness before, but never like
this. 'Robert, you mustn't——'

'Mustn't what?' he demanded as she paused.

'Mustn't torture yourself,' she whispered. 'It
doesn't do any good—it only makes things worse.
And it hurts me too, to see you so unhappy.'

'Does it?' His lips twisted. 'And do you think of
that when you go swinging off across the hills with
your friend Andrew? Do you think of me then,
imprisoned here? Oh—what's the use?' He swung
away again and Fenella's heart ached at the desolation in his voice. 'Obviously I have to get used to
it. Give up trying to walk again—it's futile anyway.
The doctors are right, I'm here for the rest of my life
and I can only hope to hell it isn't going to be a long
one!' He flung her a tortured glance. 'And now it's
getting late. Bed for both of us.' Again, his mouth
twisted. 'Call John for me, would you? You see—
I'm worse than a baby—at least babies grow up and
learn how to put themselves to bed.'

Fenella stared at him, and then felt something
snap inside her. During the past hour—the past
days, weeks—she had been subject to so many
changing influences, so many disturbing thoughts
and sensations. Suddenly, she could bear it no
longer. She came to her feet and stood looking down
at him, her eyes blazing, hands clenched into fists at
her side, breathing rapidly with fierce emotion.

'There you go again!' she exclaimed. 'Being sorry for yourself! And do you know something—I'm tired of it. *Everyone's* tired of it! All right, what's happened to you is dreadful—but anyone would think you were the only person in the world to have anything dreadful happen to you. And you're not. You don't have a monopoly in misfortune. What about me? I still don't know anything about myself—I've lost twenty-six years and it doesn't look as if I'll ever get them back. What about Mrs Bennett? She had to watch her husband die of cancer—don't you think *that* was dreadful? And it's happening all the time, every day, to someone or other. Even Walter, the gardener, has lost his wife. Do you think he suffers any less than you do, simply because he doesn't have a university education and a degree? Of course he doesn't—and neither does he sit around bewailing his ill fortune. It's part of life—and what's happened to you and to me is part of life too. We have to *accept* it and just get on with our lives as they are.' She stopped, astonished by her own words. Robert was watching her, a curious expression on his face. 'Well, that's what I'm trying to do anyway,' she finished lamely. 'And now I'm going to bed. I'll call John on my way. And if you want to know what I think about that——'

'I suspect I'm going to hear it, in any case,' he said a trifle grimly.

'Well, I think you're being most unfair to John, working as late as this. He has to stay up late whether he wants to or not, just because you've got the bit between your teeth. I think you should consider him a bit more. In fact, it wouldn't hurt you to consider anyone at all, just for once—you might find thinking about other people a refreshing change.'

She stopped again, realising suddenly that she was trembling violently, and turned to pick up her bag. Robert put out a hand but she ignored it. There was so much more she wanted to say, but she was suddenly overwhelmed by exhaustion and she didn't think he was likely to listen anyway. She looked at his face and remembered the kiss they had shared, the dizzying emotions she had experienced, and felt a sudden sting in her eyes. If only things could be different. If only. . .

'I'm sorry,' she said abruptly. 'I shouldn't have spoken to you like that. I'm going to bed—I'll call John.' And she turned on her heel and left the room without another glance at the motionless figure in the wheelchair.

Upstairs in her room, she sat on her bed for a long time, trying to control her shaking body and the painful tears that threatened to take her by storm. She could still feel his kiss on her lips, burning the tender flesh. She could see the look in his eyes as he'd listened to her tirade. She longed with a fierce, helpless longing to go back, to take him in her arms, cradle his head against her breast and find the harmony that she had so often felt awaited them, only to be shattered by Robert's bitter repudiation of his disability.

At last she got up, undressed, washed and lay down beneath the light, summerweight duvet. But it was a long, sleepless night that she spent, tossing in the bed that had once seemed so comfortable and

was now so lonely. And even when she did doze,
fitfully, towards morning, it was only to feel again
the strength of Robert's arms around her, the reeling
sensation of his kiss.

And to feel again that strange, fleeting glimpse of
something more—something deeply right, almost
familiar, that she'd experienced as she'd let her
mouth follow his and entered for a moment a world
that had been inexplicably denied her.

For the next few days, Robert and Fenella worked
together with a polite formality which drove like a
sword into her heart. Time after time, she would
look up, steeling herself to say something—but
always the ice in his eyes drove her back into herself,
wordless and unhappy.

She tried, on the first morning, to apologise for
her outburst. But Robert merely heard her out in
silence, then inclined his head before reaching out
to draw some papers towards him.

'That's quite all right, Fenella. We were both tired
and probably said things we didn't mean. And no
doubt you were absolutely right to remind me of my
duties towards my employees—it isn't fair of me to
keep either you or John up so late.'

Fenella bit her lip. But he was right too—she *was*
his employee. And no more than that, she told
herself, in spite of that kiss.

'I just wanted to say——' she began, but he cut in
with that deadly politeness that left her helpless.

'I think you've said all that's necessary, don't you?
And now, if you don't mind. . .' His glance
reminded her that she was here to work, and Fenella

bent her head over her notebook, feeling the scarlet colour wash into her cheeks.

Perhaps he would thaw when the work was over and they were sharing a meal together, or listening to the music they had discovered they both enjoyed, or reading quietly in the soft light of the evening. She was surprised, when she began to think about it, to realise just how many quiet occupations they enjoyed sharing. And they had never needed to discuss how they would spend the evening. It was as if both knew by instinct what the other would enjoy—as if they had known each other for a long, long time. Long enough to see clearly into each other's hearts.

But even that thought brought its own pain, as she acknowledged that there would be many other, more active interests to share if only Robert were able to leave the wheelchair that bound him. Walking, as she and Andrew walked together; swimming; playing squash and tennis, both games he had admitted to loving before his accident; skating and even skiing, his great love, which Fenella had never tried—how did she know that?—but loved to watch on TV.

But Robert did not thaw. Instead, his coolness chilling the air, he would retreat after dinner, back to his study, making it clear that company was not required. And Fenella, miserable and lonely, would listen to music without hearing a note, stare at her book without seeing a word and stare out into the twilit garden without registering a single shrub or flower.

At the end of the week, Robert finished the page he was working on and then glanced up at her.

'You realise we've almost finished this book, don't you?' he said.

'Have—have we? But I thought——'

'You thought I'd be wanting you to go to London—maybe even Paris. Well, it's not necessary.' His eyes were cool, cynical. 'Sorry about that. It's turned out to be rather dull after all, hasn't it?'

'I didn't say that,' she protested. 'And it hasn't been dull at all—it's been fascinating.' She hesitated, then said, 'I suppose you'll be thinking of a new book now.'

'Probably,' he said dismissively. 'But you needn't worry about that. I won't be ready to start for quite a while.'

Fenella stared at him. 'But——'

'Oh, don't worry,' he said. 'I'll do the right thing by you.'

'Robert, please. You know I——'

'No,' he said curtly. 'Don't. Don't say anything. Just finish what you're doing and then—go. Take some time off. Go and find your friend Andrew and spend the evening with him. I mean it,' he added as she stared at him in silent appeal. 'I don't want to see you here this evening. You've worked hard enough.'

Fenella opened her mouth and then closed it. Very well, if that's the way you want it, she thought angrily. I've tried hard enough, heaven knows. But if you're determined to go on being stubborn—if you've really made up your mind we can't even be friends. . .

With a swift movement, she gathered her papers together and slipped them into a file. She fitted the top on to her pen, dropped it into her bag and stood up.

'In that case,' she said, and her voice was as cool as his, 'I think I'll go right away. There really isn't any more I can do at present. No doubt you'll let me have the final draft to type as soon as you think it's ready. And, if you're sure you don't want me any more, I'll do as you suggest and go and ring Andrew. There's a special folk dance on in the village tonight—he asked me to go but I thought we'd be too busy.' She gave him a long, straight look that revealed nothing of the turmoil going on inside her. 'I expect I'll be quite late back,' she added, deliberately and quite unnecessarily, and turned to walk out.

At the door, she paused for a second. Her heart ached in her breast; she wanted to turn back, to run to the chair, to kneel beside it and take his head against her breast, letting her fingers tangle in the thick black hair, letting her lips smooth out the bitter lines. She wanted to tell him that she loved him.

But she could not make that final, tiny movement of her head which would have allowed her eyes to meet his.

Robert did not appear next morning, and as Fenella worked alone in the study she was brought her coffee by Mrs Bennett, together with a letter. She looked at it in surprise.

'It's from the professor,' Mrs Bennett explained

awkwardly. 'He asked me to give it to you with your coffee. He's gone away for a while.'

'Gone away?' Fenella echoed. 'But how—when? He never mentioned it last night.'

'Early this morning, Miss Fenella. He got John to call him early and they went off very quiet before eight.' The housekeeper looked disturbed. 'He was in a funny mood too—gone very quiet and determined, like. I've never seen him like that before.'

With a feeling of sudden dread, Fenella slit open the long white envelope. Inside was a short letter, and a cheque. She looked at the cheque and felt a surge of bitterness. As a pay-off, it was generous indeed—but why? What had she done? What was Robert up to, for heaven's sake?

'He says he's going abroad for treatment,' she said slowly, her mind dazed. 'To Switzerland. This—this is three months' salary in lieu of notice. But—I don't understand. He never said yesterday that. . .'

'He didn't say anything to me, either. But there it is, he's gone and I'm to pack up the rest of his things and send them on when he lets me know his address.' Mrs Bennett looked compassionately at Fenella's white face. 'I'm sorry, miss. There wasn't any way of breaking it gently.'

'No.' Fenella looked at the letter again. It was brief, almost terse, written as he had spoken to her for the past few days. It shouldn't, she supposed, have come as a shock—he'd tried to prepare her, telling her that the book was finished, hinting that it was time she left. But she'd thought—somehow, she'd thought. . . Fenella rested her head on her hand. What *had* she thought, after all? What could she have thought?

He must have been planning this, for days if not longer. Weeks, perhaps. She remembered the letters from Switzerland. Had they been from this clinic he mentioned? Had he been in communication with the doctors there for a long time, without mentioning it to her, or to John or even Sam?

He must have known he was going to go away. Had he known what it would do to her? Had he even suspected the growing feeling in her heart, the sense that they belonged together, that in some other life they had found harmony and love? Or had it all been a figment of her own imagination—a wish, projected by her loneliness? A mere shadow of something that she had thought could be real and solid?

Impatiently, she shook her head. No. The truth was that Fenella simply wasn't important to him at all. He hadn't told her about his trip abroad for treatment because he didn't see it as being any of her business. Clearly, it had been arranged for some time. The book being almost finished, it was only common sense to let her go, to start her life again as she'd declared last night she was ready to do.

And he'd been more than generous in the matter of her salary.

'Well,' she said, trying to collect herself together, 'I suppose I'd better just finish the work I'm doing now and—and pack up.' Her voice quivered suddenly. The future was bleak, like a cold wintry sky stretching out of sight. 'I'll be sorry to leave here,' she said and thought of never seeing Cowleaze again, never knowing it in the golden Cotswold autumn, the windswept winter or the spring, fresh and bright with primroses in the hedgerows and bluebell-filled woods. In the short time she had been here, the house and its surroundings had wound itself around her heart.

As, she recognised with a cold, sharp pain, had Robert Milburn.

She loved him. She loved his home. She wanted to be here with him, and he was turning her away, without so much as a goodbye.

'We'll be sorry to see you go,' Mrs Bennett answered her. 'It's been a real pleasure having you about the place. And Walter and me—well, we reckon you did the professor a lot of good. He's the kind of man that could suffer a lot in his mind, if you understand me—he needs someone to take him out of himself, help him enjoy life. And you could do that, just by coming into the room he was in.'

'Do you really think so?' Fenella smiled wryly. 'I sometimes think I make his depression worse. And I'm sure I didn't help him much a few nights ago.' She told Mrs Bennett how she had stormed at him. 'I said he was too full of self-pity to think of anyone else,' she concluded ruefully. 'It's not really surprising he's sacked me, is it?'

Mrs Bennett pursed her lips. 'Maybe, maybe not. If you ask me, it was just what he needed. But that's men all over—my husband was just the same. Get a bit of a headache or a cut finger and he was worrying like a baby—yet, when he got something really wrong with him, nobody could have been braver. Well, there it is.' She picked up her tray. 'There's no dealing with them at times. Anyway, I don't see as there's any call for you to go rushing off, Miss Fenella. You finish what you're doing, if you think you should, and take your time over it. He can't expect you to pack up and go all in a few minutes. And, since he's not here himself, I don't see as it can make any difference when you go.'

Fenella smiled and thanked her, but her grey eyes were thoughtful as the housekeeper went out of the room. It was all very well for Mrs Bennett to talk like that, and what she said was perfectly reasonable—Fenella had work to finish and there was no reason why she should rush it. And with Robert not here. . .

But with Robert not here, what was the point in staying?

Fenella sat at her desk, drinking her coffee without tasting it, telling herself over and over again that she'd been lucky, that she'd been tremendously fortunate to have had such a job to ease herself gradually back into the world. She'd lived and worked in a beautiful place, doing something she'd enjoyed and found totally fascinating, for a man she liked and admired even while he was at his most difficult. She'd made a good friend in Andrew, and she had sufficient money to be able to go back to her London flat and take her time in finding a new position.

Yes, she'd been lucky. Really lucky.

And now there was nothing left for her but to go back to London. Pick up the pieces. And start again.

CHAPTER SIX

FENELLA let herself into her flat and looked around her.

It wasn't so very different from that day when she'd come here with Sam Whitman to collect her clothes. She hadn't made any alterations—there had been no real need. That other Fenella, still unremembered, had decorated the rooms and furnished them to her taste, and although there was still a tinge of unfamiliarity about them—as if the real owner might at any moment walk in through the door—she had settled in and begun to think of it as home.

There really wasn't anything else to do, after all. There was nowhere else she could think of as home.

With a determined movement, Fenella walked across to the window and drew the curtains, trying as she did so to banish the picture of Cowleaze that had immediately risen in her mind. Cowleaze was *not* her home, nor ever would be. She must stop thinking about it—and about Robert Milburn.

With a hopeless movement of her shoulders, Fenella dropped into a chair and stared unseeingly across the room. Was she ever going to be free of this—this obsession? Because that was what it was. A constant, persistent presence in her mind and heart. And nothing she did seemed able to banish it.

In the months since she had left Cowleaze and

returned to her flat, Fenella had found peace an elusive commodity. At first, bruised and unhappy after her dismissal, she had wanted nothing more than to crawl into a hole and hide from everyone. All her insecurity had returned, all her new-found confidence drained away. She had spent many bitter nights crying futile tears, and many desolate days in bleak solitude, staring from her window at the children playing in the square, her mind ranging uselessly back to those first moments in hospital. Trying to pull away the dark cobwebs that shrouded her memory, trying in vain to remember what and who she had been before that second lonely birth.

And, inevitably, such thoughts had brought with them the memory of Robert. So many memories: memories of him in his wheelchair, chasing the ball the first time she had seen him; wheeling himself around the garden at Cowleaze; driving himself frustratedly back and forth across the carpet as if he wanted to be up and pacing the room. His eyes, burning with a passion that turned their steel to flame, cold with an ice that froze her own yearning heart.

And more elusive memories, memories that could not be caught and held. Little more than impressions—of strong arms that held her in a powerful, yet gentle, grip; fingers that touched and pressed and stroked; a body that was firm and warm and fitted its shape to hers. . .

And, with every such memory, a final blank wall, like a curtain, had dropped heavily and inexorably over her eyes so that she turned away in despair and knew that she would never reach the truth that lay behind it.

I can't go on like this, Fenella had thought one morning. I'll go mad if I don't do something. Take charge of my own life. Send these memories back where they belong—to the past. And *forget* Robert Milburn.

And, as if it were meant, her eyes had fallen to a magazine she had been reading the evening before, and she'd remembered the advertisement she had been reading.

'Assertiveness Training,' she had read again. 'Don't be a Doormat. Take Charge of Your Own Life.'

That's it, she'd thought. That's what I need to do. Take charge of my life. *Then* I'll be able to forget Robert Milburn.

She had applied immediately to join a class, and had started the following week. She had learnt to cope with every kind of circumstance—how to return a pair of substandard shoes to a shop and insist on her money back, how to deal with sexual harassment at work, how to handle a potential mugging. She had learnt to smile at opposition and get her own way, how to manage her own feelings when her temper threatened to get the better of her, how to turn a disappointment to positive advantage. She had learnt to be calm, cool and positive in any situation. She had even learnt to come to terms with her loss of memory, and to admit to it without feeling like a freak.

But she had not learnt to forget Robert Milburn.

If ever she could have used a loss of memory, she thought bitterly, this was the time.

Now the autumn, so golden at Cowleaze, had passed and winter was approaching. The November nights were dark and cold, with only the lights of shops and theatres to brighten them. But Fenella, coming home from work among a thrusting, pushing crowd of commuters, found little pleasure in the bustle. More and more, she found herself longing for the quiet peace of the countryside, the earth carpeted in tawny leaves and rich with the smell of rain, the buds already black on the tips of ash trees.

She had made friends in the office where she was currently working, and, occasionally, she would go with one or two of them to the country for a day at the weekend. They would catch a train for Sussex or Berkshire, getting off at some small station and walking back across country until they could pick up a return train further back along the line. Then they would come back to her flat or the one shared by the other girls, and make supper—toasted cheese, perhaps, or spaghetti—and lie on the big sofa or in armchairs, feeling pleasantly exhausted and listening to records.

But, try as she might, the moment could not be postponed forever—the moment when she was finally alone. And, as if it had been waiting for its opportunity, the picture of Robert Milburn would immediately slide into her mind. Grim-faced, with sombre grey eyes and a new harshness to his jaw; watching her with a sardonic twist to his chiselled lips, as if he knew every thought she had.

Why should the mere thought of him have the

power to twist her heart, as if he had taken it in his fingers and caressed it into helplessness?

But allowing such despondent thoughts to invade her mind wasn't allowed. And one way in which Fenella had learnt to handle these moments was to keep busy. She jumped up from her chair and went to the window again. It was a fine, clear night—and it was the night that the Oxford Street Christmas lights were due to be switched on. Some of the girls from the office where she was currently working were going to see them and had invited her to go along too. Well—why not? It would pass the time, if nothing else. It would get her through one more long, lonely evening.

And a little nearer to a long, lonely night. . .

It was late when Fenella returned. After the lights had been switched on, she and the others had walked the length of Oxford Street, admiring the effects and looking at the colourful displays in the windows of the big stores. Then they had decided to go for a meal and had taken a long time to choose a restaurant. By the time they had eaten, it was after ten, and they sat over their coffee for another half-hour or more while cheerful customers came and went, and the waiters bustled to and fro without apparently noticing the group of laughing girls in the corner.

It had been a cheerful, giggling evening. And as Fenella paid off her taxi at the steps of the house where she had her flat, she was still smiling, glad that she'd decided to go.

A tall dark figure detached itself from the shadows

and she gave a little scream, then hastily dragged together the memories of her assertiveness training.

'Who are you?' she demanded. 'What are you doing here?'

'Don't get in a panic, Fenella,' drawled a familiar, deep voice. 'I'm not going to hurt you.' He stepped a little closer and she drew back, scarcely able to believe her ears. 'I know it's late,' he said quietly. 'And you may well have other plans. But I've come a long way to see you. Can I come in?'

Fenella stared at him, unable to speak, unbelieving. It must be a mistake—an illusion. It couldn't be. . . Then he moved, and the light from the street lamp fell across his face. She saw the thick black hair, the straight brows, the finely shaped lips. She saw the moonlight glimmer of his eyes.

'*Robert*. . .' she whispered. 'But—but you're—you're *walking*. . .'

'I told you I would,' he said briefly. 'Didn't you believe me?'

Fenella shook her head wordlessly. She could not analyse her feelings—hadn't she wept over this man, endured hours of lonely torment because she had lost him? Hadn't she told herself she was better off without him, that she never wanted to see him again? Hadn't she longed for his presence beside her, while at the same time she tried, uselessly, to forget him?

And now he was here, standing tall before her as she had seen him only in dreams. The lights of the night glinting on shadow-black hair, gleaming in eyes the colour of moonlight. And she wanted to step forward, to fling herself into his arms—even while she drew back in the fear of what he might do to her heart.

I've tried so hard, she thought as she gazed up at him. I've tried to make my own life—and tonight I thought I just might be getting somewhere. And now you come back—to tell me what? That you can walk again? So that you can walk right out of my life?

'I want to talk to you,' he said.

'Do we have anything to talk about?' She found her key and went slowly up the steps, too numb now to care whether or not he followed her. She fitted the key into the lock and felt him close behind her.

'Fenella. . .' If it had been any other man, she would have sworn there was a note of appeal in the low voice. But not Robert. Not proud, arrogant Robert Milburn.

'May I come in?'

She shrugged and did not answer. The door swung open and she walked through, and knew that he was following.

Upstairs, she opened her own door and walked across to the window. The night was still clear. The square below was empty except for an old man walking his dog. She looked down and thought how peaceful it looked. She had come here for peace, for strength. And now Robert was back. To shatter her peace; to drain away that precious strength.

'And now, please, can I come in?'

Turning from the window, she looked across the room at the man who stood just inside the door.

It was as if she were seeing him for the first time. He was even taller than she had supposed, his body lean as a whippet, his face thinner than she remembered with the grey eyes brilliant in hollow dark sockets. He was watching her with a hunger in his face that caused her to back away. Instantly, his expression changed.

'I'm sorry,' he said. 'I've startled you, coming here like this. But it's my first day in London. . . I wanted to see you as soon as possible.'

'The treatment you went away for,' Fenella said stupidly. 'It worked.'

His mouth curved in a faint smile. 'As you see. Not that you could call it "treatment"—it was mostly bloody hard work, on my part. But I'd made up my mind to do it.' He shrugged slightly. 'Some men make up their minds to climb Everest.'

And that's probably easier, Fenella thought. But even as she acknowledged her admiration for his courage and perseverance she was aware of a flicker of anger at the way he had left her.

'Well, I'm glad it was successful,' she said coolly. 'And now that you've seen me, I expect you'd like to go again. Or do you want a drink first?'

His eyebrows rose. 'Is that intended as a dismissal? I've only just arrived.'

'I really can't see why you had to come here at this time of night, Robert. Couldn't you have waited until tomorrow? Or at least phoned?'

'I had an idea,' he said slowly, 'that you might be pleased to see me.'

Fenella slapped her bag down on to a table. 'Oh, *did* you? Now, I wonder why you should have thought that? After the way you walked out——' she bit her lip '—I'm sorry, after the way you *left* before, why should you think I'd *ever* want to see you again? Don't you realise how that hurt?' she demanded, her voice quivering infuriatingly. 'Don't you know what I felt like, finding that you'd gone? And leaving me a cheque in lieu of notice! It was nothing more than an insult.'

To her astonishment, Robert smiled. 'An insult?' he murmured. 'Now, why should you see it that way? You were my secretary, I was dismissing you simply to suit my own purposes—yes, I admit that—so what could be more fair than that I should give you three months' salary? It seems eminently fair to me—and would to you, too, if you'd been looking on me simply as your employer.'

'And how else do you suppose I was looking on you?' Fenella asked coldly, and his smile widened. He moved towards her, slowly. There was no trace of unsteadiness in his walk; he looked as sleek and as purposeful as a leopard closing in for the kill.

He stopped inches away from her.

'I hoped you were looking on me in the same way as I've always looked on you,' he said softly, and the dark timbre of his voice sent a thrill chasing across her skin. 'As something more than an employer. Something more than a friend.'

Fenella gazed up at him. She could feel a pulse fluttering wildly in her throat. His nearness was like a heat on her skin, drawing up each tiny hair to stand erect. She tried to breathe and wondered if she had lost the knack.

'Don't you see why I had to go away?' he murmured, and lifted one hand to trail a gentle fingertip down the side of her neck. 'What did I have to offer you, trapped in that damned wheelchair? What could I do or say, when I couldn't even follow you out of a room? But I knew I couldn't stand living so close to you much longer without some kind of explosion. And I couldn't risk losing you.' His fingers were moving slowly just under the edge of her collar, barely touching her skin, yet the shock of each tiny movement radiated through her body. 'I had to get away—I had to be able to walk again before I came back. There was no "treatment", Fenella—just a lot of hard work and determination. But I made it.' He spread his arms wide. 'As you can see, I can now stand alone and walk without sticks. Not far just yet—but I'll improve. And you'll walk with me, Fenella, with *me*—do you understand what I mean?'

Fenella shook her head. She wanted to refute his words. Why should she walk with him anywhere? But the words would not come. She gazed up at him, her eyes held by his, her lips parted, and remembered the kiss they had shared at Cowleaze.

As if he was remembering it too, Robert's gaze fell to her mouth. He bent his head and touched her lips very gently with his. Then he gathered her in his arms, drawing her against him, and his mouth was firm on hers, exploring, shaping, his tongue probing, and his hand was on her breast, caressing, teasing the nipple into hardness, covering it with his palm and gentling it with his fingers.

When he finally took his mouth from hers, Fenella was weak and dizzy. She leaned against him. Her anger had vanished, and she knew that he had been right to come back. Without him, she had been only half alive.

'I love you, Fenella,' he said quietly. 'You know that now, don't you? You understand why I had to do what I did.'

She shook her head. 'You didn't have to go away. You could have told me then—that night.'

'No. Not while I was in that wheelchair.'

'It wouldn't have made any difference,' she protested, but again he shook his head. He took her hands and led her across to the sofa, and they sat down, their bodies turned towards each other.

'Why should you think that would have mattered?' she asked. 'I was in love with you then—I didn't realise it, but I was. Your being in a wheelchair wouldn't have stopped me loving you.'

'But it stopped me. I don't think you realised just how much I hated that contraption, Fenella, how I longed to escape from it. All the time I was in it, I felt only half a man. I didn't even know if I *could* love a woman—how could I ask you to marry me? How could I ask you to make promises, to tie yourself down? I had to be sure everything would be right for you. That's why I went away so suddenly.' He paused, then added, 'I also had to make sure of your feelings. There was young Andrew—you might very well have begun to fall for him. I had to give you time.' He stopped again and said, painfully, 'I still don't know for certain. He may still be around— you may still be seeing him. Perhaps you've been with him this evening——'

Fenella shook her head. 'I don't see very much of Andrew. His job keeps him too busy. And there's only friendship between us anyway. That's all there ever was, Robert.'

'You're sure?'

She hesitated. 'On my part, yes,' she said at last. 'I think Andrew would like it to go further. But it never has. He's never been anything but a very good friend to me.' She looked into Robert's eyes and added quietly, 'I do mean that, Robert. Andrew isn't the boy you think he is. He's a very sensitive man and the girl he marries will be a lucky woman. But it won't be me.'

'You're damned right it won't,' he growled as he swept her into his arms again. 'It won't be you, because you're already spoken for, Fenella. You're going to marry me—and as soon as possible. Is that understood?'

Fenella opened her mouth to protest, but it was immediately claimed by his searching lips. And this time the kiss was deeper and even more intimate than before. As if he needed to know every tiny particle of her flesh, his mouth searched and explored her lips from corner to corner, tasting the sweetness of the tender inner flesh, his tongue pressing with gentle insistence against hers. And Fenella found herself responding, answering his pressure with her own, letting her own lips and teeth nip gently in return, letting her tongue move and entangle with his in a sweet rhythm that seemed to call to her body to move against him in ecstatic surrender. With a sigh, she let herself slip back on the cushions, felt the weight of him upon her and stretched herself under him. She felt him run a hand down the length of her body, from shoulder to thigh,

and turned herself closer to him, lifting her head as
he removed his mouth from hers, arching her neck
so that he could trace the pulse that beat so frantically in her throat.

'It's understood, isn't it?' he muttered, and she
remembered dimly what he had just asked—or,
rather, stated. A proposal of marriage—was that
what it had been? But there was no need for such a
proposal, was there? Because it had all happened
before, it had been understood in that other life and
nothing had happened, even death and rebirth, to
alter that.

'Oh, Robert,' she murmured, 'what's been happening to us? Why has it taken so long?'

He kissed her again, drawing the sweetness from
her mouth, and then dropped his head to her breasts
which were somehow naked now, the buttons of her
shirt open and her flimsy bra no defence against his
onslaught. 'You know why, my darling. But it's all
right now—everything's all right now. And we'll be
married as soon as possible.' He lifted himself above
her and looked down into her face, his fingers tracing
the line of her brows. 'You'll have no need to worry
or be frightened again—ever.'

Fenella reached up and drew him down to her
again, wanting to experience again the kiss that
drove all thought from her head, all emotions but
one from her heart. Her body's yearning increased,
she twisted against him, whimpering with a desire
that was growing too rapidly for her control. Her
fingers moved and tightened convulsively on his
shoulders, his back, his neck, and all the frustration
of those long, arid months, months when she had

not known who she was or what her life had been, increased inside her, driving her on to the only release she could ever know. Whispering her pleas, she clung to him. And then she heard his whisper in her ear.

'Do you want me to go, Fenella?'

'No,' she breathed. 'Oh, no, no. . .'

'Do you want me to stay?' The murmur was like velvet in her ear.

'Yes. . .'

With a swift, decisive movement, he lifted himself away from her and took her up in his arms. He carried her quickly across the room, opened the bedroom door and laid her gently on the bed. Then, slowly and with infinite gentleness, he undressed her. But, gentle as he was, the light, brushing touch of his fingertips seemed to burn her tender skin with instant fire and she moaned as the heat of desire mounted within her. She held up her arms, wanting him against her, close, close, close.

For a few moments, he left her. Fenella lay with her eyes closed, feeling the wild beat of her heart. And then he was beside her, his skin cool against hers, bringing a shock more violent than any she had known yet. And then, as he touched her and laid his lips once more against her mouth, she felt memory strike like a blow to the head. She twisted sharply away, gasping, and tore herself from his arms.

'*You*!' she whispered, staring at him. 'You, Robert—it was you all the time. . .'

She could see the instant understanding in his eyes, and she shook her head like a dog coming out of the water. And, indeed, she felt that she had just

emerged from some deep dark lake, as if she had
been drowning and was only now coming to the
surface.

'You. . .' She breathed again, and raised a shaking hand to her head.

Robert gazed down at her, his eyes dark as the
shadows that surrounded them.

'Have you remembered?'

'Yes. . . I don't know. . .' Her voice was dazed.
'My mind is full of pictures—voices—I can't sort
them out. . . I don't know what I remember. There's
so much, and it's all mixed up. My mother and
father—school—college—Jeremy, someone called
Jeremy. . .' She shuddered. 'And you—you. You
were there all the time. You were there when it
happened.' She flung a wild glance around the room
and took in a sharp breath. 'It happened *here*, didn't
it? That last night—it was here, and we were—we
were——'

'We were making love,' he said. 'Fenella, don't
force it. Just lie quietly here with me and let it come
back naturally. And don't be afraid.' His hands were
on her now, drawing her close to him in the bed,
calming her. 'There's nothing to be afraid of now,'
he said softly. 'We're here, we're together and
nothing's going to happen. Just lie quietly against
me, and remember, and then it'll all be over.'

'I'm afraid,' Fenella whispered. 'Robert, I'm
afraid to remember.'

'Perhaps you are for the moment.' His fingers
caressed her with a tenderness that made her want
to weep. 'But the memories are coming back now,
my darling—you can't avoid them. All you can do is

let it happen in its own time, and tell yourself there's nothing to be afraid of now—and trust me. Talk to me; tell me what you remember.'

They lay very quietly for a while. And then Fenella took a long, shivering breath, and nodded.

'It's all right, Robert. I'm ready now,' she said, and closed her eyes as the memories poured into her mind.

CHAPTER SEVEN

THE memories came at Fenella from every side, like a rain of bullets, each striking her with a force that left her gasping. Pictures swarmed before her eyes: herself as a child, holding on to someone's hand. . .as a teenager, giggling with her friends, trying new make-up, wearing jeans that looked old when they were bought, listening to pop songs. . .as a woman, looking into someone's eyes, feeling the first heartbeat of love. And pain. The pain of loneliness.

And, past all that, like a great black cloud emptying itself into her mind, a fear and horror that even now made her turn her head sharply away, afraid to face whatever lurked in her still frightened memory.

Yet she knew that now there was no escape. It was there, recalled in total, waiting in ambush for the moment when her guard was relaxed and she had no choice but to remember, in all its horrifying detail.

Robert was watching her. His eyes were sombre and Fenella knew that he was aware of what had happened to her.

'Do you remember everything?' he asked quietly, and she turned her head on the pillow.

'Everything. . . That's a big question, Robert.' Her voice came in a whisper, like someone in shock.

'There's so much. . . New things all the time. I need
to sort it out. I need to think.'

'You need to be alone,' he stated, and she turned
at once, her eyes terrified.

'No! No, don't leave me. I can't be alone, I'm
afraid, I——' She stopped, trembling in his arms,
and buried her face against his bare shoulder.
'Robert, I've go to think, to sort out all the memories—they're confused, I don't know which comes
first or where I am now. But I want you with me. . .if
you'll stay. Will you. . .please?'

He smiled, and she saw to her astonishment that
there was relief as well as compassion in his eyes.
And something else, too; something that she
believed—hoped—was love. But she wouldn't know
that until she had come to the end of her remembering, for Robert was an important part of her
memories.

And as she thought that, she knew too that he was
deeply involved in that last memory. . .the one that
filled her with such nameless horror, the one that
waited, lurking in the shadows of her mind.

He shifted slightly in the bed, moving to settle her
more closely in his arms, and she felt his nakedness
against her and marvelled that they could lie so close
without passion.

But the moment for passion had passed. It would
come again, of that she had no doubt. But now was
the time for memories, and she lay back against the
pillows, letting his body warm hers, and—in the
knowledge that she was safe—allowed them to flow
gently into her mind, taking and looking at them
one by one and then laying them aside like old and

comfortable clothes as she drew nearer and nearer to the last one; the one that had closed her mind as if forever, and denied her access to all her previous life.

It had all started, she thought, on the day that she had met Jeremy Sands. Until then, her life had followed a fairly ordinary, normal pattern—educated at one of the few remaining girls-only grammar schools, followed by a course in librarianship at the local polytechnic college and a job in the library of a teachers' training college about thirty miles away from her home. Just too far to travel each day, so she'd found herself a tiny flat near by and gone home most weekends. She had had boyfriends, of course, but there had been nobody special—until Jeremy.

Fenella remembered the first day she had seen him. She had been sorting out some newly arrived books with one of the other girls, and had glanced up to see him wander in and stand hesitantly by the desk. A shaft of sunlight, coming in through one of the high windows, had illuminated his fair hair, turning it the colour of ripe corn. The moment was as vivid as if it had happened yesterday.

'Hell-o,' the girl with her said softly. 'That looks like the new English lecturer—I heard he was quite a dish. Shall we toss for it?'

Fenella smiled, but her heart was behaving oddly, almost skipping, and her breath was coming quickly. She saw the man look across at them and felt a twinge of panic. 'No, it's all right, Jenny—you go. I'll carry on sorting these books.'

'You're mad,' Jenny muttered, and rose to her feet with alacrity. 'I always suspected it. Well, don't say I never gave you a chance.' She went across to the man, her best smile pinned firmly in place, and Fenella bent her head, half amused and half regretful. She had no doubt that by the time the new English lecturer was out of the library, Jenny would have a date to meet him again. Unless he was married. . .but something told Fenella that he wasn't, and her heart gave another of its odd little skips.

She continued with her work, but every few moments her eyes seemed to peep of their own accord through her long lashes at the couple who stood earnestly talking together across the quiet room. Then she saw Jenny leave the man and come back towards her. But he didn't move. He simply stood there, as if waiting, his eyes following Jenny. And coming to rest on Fenella.

'Oh, Fenella,' Jenny said in elaborately casual tones as she approached. 'Mr Sands wants a book from the reference room. I'm just going in to show him around, all right?' Coming nearer, she dropped her voice and murmured, 'Not that he doesn't look as if he knows his way around already. I told you you were mad, Fenella—he's a real dish. His name's Jeremy and he's single and looking for a cottage to rent. Things are looking up around here!'

Fenella laughed. 'And do you know his star sign, personal mantra and favourite colour as well?' she teased. 'Jenny, you're incorrigible.'

'I know. But it's fun.' Jenny winked, went back to the tall man who stood waiting, still in that shaft of sunlight, and led him into the small room where they kept books which were not allowed out on loan to the students. Fenella watched them go, saw the door close firmly behind them and went back to her work. If she knew anything at all about Jenny, it would be some time before they emerged. . .

In fact, she was never sure just how long the two were in there, for shortly after that a flurry of students arrived and had to be dealt with, and then she had a query from one of the lecturers. With one thing and another, by the time she drew breath again it was almost time to close and Jenny was beside her with the books, which she had finished sorting, and Jeremy Sands was nowhere to be seen.

'Oh, he went ages ago,' Jenny said airily, in response to Fenella's question. 'There was a cottage he wanted to look at—I told you he was looking for somewhere to rent, didn't I?'

'And when's your first date?'

Jenny looked shocked. 'Honestly, Fenella, what sort of girl do you think I am? Do you really think I'd go out with a man the first time I met him. . .? Yes, you know darned well I would!' She grinned. 'Actually, he never asked me for one—I must be slipping. As a matter of fact, he seemed to be more interested in you.'

'In *me*?' Fenella stared at her in astonishment, her heart kicking suddenly. 'Jenny, you're having me on.'

'I'm not. He *is* interested in you, Fel. Kept on working the conversation round to you—what was your name, where did you live, do you have a steady boyfriend. Oh, he tried not to let it be too obvious,

piled on the charm and all that, but I'm not a fool—
that man's going to be back, Fenella, and it won't
be me he goes into the reference room with, not if
he's got any say in the matter.'

Fenella gazed at her. 'But what did you say about
me?'

'Well, what do you think? Told him you were an
ogre, of course, married with six kids and a jealous
husband who's got medals for prizefighting. . .'
Jenny burst out laughing at Fenella's expression.
'You don't have to look like that! What do you *think*
I told him, for heaven's sake?'

Fenella blushed and smiled. 'Well, I don't know.
I just can't believe he would be interested in me.
Not with you opening those big blue eyes at him.
After all, we all know that gentlemen prefer
blondes.'

'Not when they're blond themselves,' Jenny
remarked thoughtfully. 'They go for the brunettes
then, for the contrast. Anyway. . .how do we know
he's a gentleman? With any luck, he isn't!'

Which two comments Fenella was to remember
later. Much later.

When it was entirely too late.

She didn't see Jeremy Sands for a few days, and,
although she glanced up every time someone came
into the library, her heart jumping, she began at last
to think that Jenny had either been mistaken or
teasing her.

Not that she was sorry, she told herself as she
went briskly about her work. Just at present, her life
suited her very well, with the occasional friendly
date with one of the two or three men who vied with

each other—not very seriously—for her company, her weekends at home and with a job she enjoyed. There was plenty going on socially at the college, and she joined in several of the groups, going on Sunday rambles in the country or attending the folk dance club and its ceilidhs.

No, she didn't want any additional complications—and she had a distinct feeling that if Jeremy Sands came into her life that was just what he would do. Bring complications.

With that decision firm in her mind, she didn't even glance up when a shadow fell across the book she was working on. It was only when a cool voice said, in amused tones, 'I suppose you wouldn't be able to help me, would you? I'm looking for a book. . .' that her heart began to kick, and she froze into absolute stillness.

She had never heard his voice before. But she knew it at once.

Jeremy Sands.

Slowly, she lifted her eyes and looked straight into his. Dark, sapphire-blue. Direct. Challenging. . . intoxicating.

'I'm sorry?' she managed to croak out at last. 'A—a book? Oh—yes—we've got plenty of books. . .' She floundered to a stop, knowing that she sounded ridiculous, that her face was scarlet, and looked down again hastily, unable to bear the amusement she saw in his eyes. Oh, Jenny, where are you now? she thought desperately. I can't cope with this. . . But Jenny was nowhere to be seen, and she was here with Jeremy Sands and he was looking at her as if he could see right into her mind.

But when he spoke again his voice wasn't amused any longer. It was warm and friendly and when, somehow, she found the strength to look up at him again, she saw that his eyes were warm too. As if he found something immensely likeable about her.

'It's a new book, Fenella,' he said, but somehow he seemed to be telling her something quite different. 'You don't mind if I call you that, do you? Your assistant—Janey?—told me your name the other day. She thought it would be coming in soon.' He told her the name of the book. 'I don't know if it's arrived?'

'Oh—yes.' Fenella got up and led the way over to the shelf where the book had been for at least a fortnight. She smiled to herself. So Jenny had told him it would be in soon—thus giving him an excuse to call again in the next few days. And he didn't even remember her name, yet he knew Fenella's. Again, her heart moved.

'Here you are,' she said, finding the book he wanted. She held it out to him and he laid his hand on it but didn't take it from her. They stood for a moment, their fingers almost touching on the shining new cover, and she found her eyes meeting his, being held in a long look. The colour warmed her cheeks. She wanted to look away, but she couldn't. She wished he would take the book.

'You're very efficient,' he murmured. 'Almost too efficient.'

'I—I'm sorry?'

'If you hadn't been able to find it so easily,' he elaborated, 'we could have stayed behind these shelves much longer. . .and really begun to get to know each other.'

He was standing very close. She took a step back, but the shelves were immediately behind her and it was a very small step. 'Do—do you want to get to know me?' she asked breathlessly, and he laughed softly.

'I've been wanting to get to know you ever since I walked into the library—when was it? Three, four days ago? It feels more like a month!' His eyes were warm and his fingers touched hers, sending tiny, electric tingles into her palm and up the sensitive nerves of her arm. 'Fenella, you know what's happening to us, don't you?'

'No! No, I—I don't. Nothing's happening,' she denied, suddenly panic-stricken. This was going too fast. 'Please, if this is the book you want. . .' She thrust it at him, but his hand closed over hers, strong and warm, and would not let it go. 'Please,' she whispered, looking up at him imploringly.

'You know,' he muttered, and his voice was husky now, 'you really are quite irresistible.' And he bent his head to hers and just brushed her lips with his.

Fenella jumped as if she had been stung. She knocked her shoulder against the shelf behind her and three books fell to the ground. The sudden clatter sounded like an earthquake in the quiet library, and Jenny's voice called from somewhere to know if she was all right. Bending to pick the books up, Fenella called back a hasty, quavering assent and looked in desperation at Jeremy Sands, who was bending with her, his shoulders quivering with mirth.

'Please,' she said in a low voice, 'please, let me

stamp your book. I've got a lot to do. And this isn't the time or the place. . .'

'You're quite right,' he agreed gravely. He straightened and handed her books to her, his face solemn. But there was a betraying twitch pulling at the corner of his mouth, and she knew that he was close to laughter. 'So let's fix one, shall we?'

'Fix what? I don't——'

'A time and place, of course.' He walked back with her to the desk, his manner as decorous as an old gentleman's. 'I take it you agree we should.'

'I don't know.' Helplessly, she looked at him, then took his book and stamped the date in it. 'Mr Sands, I——'

'Jeremy, please.'

'I don't even know you,' she went on more firmly. 'You don't know me. We——'

'That's just the point.' He leaned his arms on the desk. 'We don't know each other. We need to get to know each other. And that means making a definite arrangement—not just hoping we'll bump into each other around the college. Now, what do you say to dinner tonight? I've found a marvellous little restaurant.'

'But I——'

'Tell me your address,' he said as if she had not interrupted. 'I'll pick you up at seven-thirty. Will that be all right?'

'But——'

'I'm only asking for one date,' he pointed out reasonably. 'Not a lifetime's commitment.'

'Yes, but——'

'And I'm quite happy to stay here until you agree,'

he went on pleasantly, and Fenella looked at him and knew he meant just that. He would stay exactly where he was until she agreed to go out with him that evening. Right through the morning—the lunch-hour—the whole afternoon.

She gave in. It wasn't so very hard, after all.

'All right. Seven-thirty.' She told him her address. 'But this doesn't mean——'

'It doesn't mean a thing,' he said cheerfully. 'Only that I'm going to pick you up at seven-thirty at your flat and take you out to dinner. It doesn't mean a thing more than that, and now I'll go and leave you to your work.' He picked up the hand she had carelessly left lying on the desk, and brushed her fingers with his lips. 'Till tonight, then. Adieu!'

With one last bright blue glance and a flash of white teeth, he was gone. And, as if materialising from nowhere, Jenny was at her side.

'Well! You didn't waste much time. Didn't I tell you it was you he was interested in? And when's the date, then?'

Fenella looked at her, sighed and then laughed reluctantly. 'Tonight. We're going out to dinner. Jenny, I don't know what's happening to me. I'd told myself I wouldn't—I'd sworn I wasn't interested. But——'

'But it wasn't true.' Jenny's blue eyes were shrewd. 'What's happening, Fel, is that you're turning out to be human, just like the rest of us. You can get smitten—and a jolly good thing too, if you ask me. You've been altogether too buttoned-up until now—comes of going to that all-girls school, I suppose. But *now*—you're about to start living. And liking it!'

'Am I?' Fenella gazed at her doubtfully. 'I hope so, Jen. I certainly hope so.'

Afterwards, she realised that from that first moment with Jeremy she hadn't stood a chance. Confident, sophisticated, utterly sure of his own magnetism, he had swept her up like a kitten waiting for a home, and like a kitten she had responded, giving him allegiance, her loyalty and her unquestioning love.

Nothing like this had ever happened to her before. She was helpless under the onslaught of his personality, bemused by the charm he knew so well how to use, overwhelmed by the power he wielded over her so effortlessly. And it never occurred to her to resent this power; rather, she welcomed it, submitting herself to it like any Victorian maiden, grateful for the attentions of this impressive and eligible male, dazzled by the new sensations that besieged her days and turned her nights into a series of feverish dreams.

'Look, Fel,' Jenny said to her one day, 'you don't have to go overboard over this hunk. I mean, anyone can see why you'd have good reason—he's the best-looking man to have come here since the year dot—but you want to *enjoy* yourself. Keep it light.' Her blue eyes were anxious. 'I get the feeling you're slipping in too deep.'

'I can't seem to stop myself,' Fenella confessed. 'Jen, I've never known anyone like him. He's—he's—well, I've just never known anyone like him,' she finished, lifting her hands helplessly.

'Good grief, you have got it bad.' Jenny hesitated, then asked bluntly, 'Are you sleeping with him?'

The colour fired into Fenella's cheeks. 'No!' Then she hesitated in her turn and Jenny nodded sagely.

'But you're not far off it, are you? He's only got to make one last move. . .oh, Fel, are you sure you know what you're doing?'

'Yes. No. I don't know. I don't seem to be sure of anything these days. I just. . .' She looked at Jenny. 'Why are you so concerned, anyway? You wouldn't hesitate if it were you.'

'No, I don't suppose I would. He turns me weak at the knees every time he comes in here, even though I know he's never even seen me, not really. But you—you're different, Fel. You don't sleep around. I know how to keep things light, fun. But for you, it's serious.' The blue eyes searched her face. 'Isn't it?'

Fenella sighed. 'Yes. It is serious.'

'So—what are you going to do?'

Fenella took a deep breath. 'For the moment— nothing. I'm going home next weekend—my parents are off to Canada for a long holiday. And then I suppose I'll just play it by ear. What else *can* I do?'

'And are you taking Jeremy home with you?'

Again Fenella paused. 'No. Not this time.' She didn't tell Jenny that, after a good deal of heart-searching, she'd invited him to go with her, and that he'd refused. Charmingly, delicately, giving her perfectly sound reasons—but the refusal had hurt, all the same. And, in a strange way, left her feeling just a little humiliated—as if she had suggested something he wasn't ready for.

Perhaps might never be ready for.

'Well,' Jenny said, 'just you be careful, Fel. You're like an innocent babe in this wicked world. I feel a hundred years old sometimes, compared with you. And I can't help feeling responsible.'

Fenella laughed. 'Don't be silly, Jen. You're not responsible. I'd have met him if you hadn't been here.'

'I know. But I encouraged you. And I know I say a lot of silly things, sometimes.' Her eyes were troubled. 'I just don't know how it is a girl grows up like you these days, Fel. Single-six schools have a lot to answer for, if you want my opinion.'

But Fenella knew that it wasn't just the school. It was the whole of her upbringing—born to parents who were already well into their forties, had long ago given up hope of having children and treated their unexpected daughter more like a precious doll than a child of the late twentieth century.

She felt herself more like the product of an earlier era, but her attitudes had been too deeply ingrained in her to be easily changed and until lately she had seen no way of 'joining the human race', as Jenny had once jokingly but all too accurately put it. But now Jeremy was changing that. Jeremy had brought feelings to life that she had never dreamed of, and with him she knew she would discover the delights that other girls talked of as naturally as they talked of having a delicious meal.

Seeing her parents off to Canada represented something of a dividing line. Until they had left, she would still not be fully grown up—she would still be their child. But with their absence, alone and wholly responsible for herself, she could begin to live an adult life. And her heart quivered at the thought.

'So,' Jeremy said when she came to his cottage on the first evening after the weekend, 'they've gone, have they? They're safely on the other side of the Atlantic. And now you needn't worry any more.'

'Worry?' She was startled by his perception.

Jeremy dropped down beside her on the sofa and laughed. His arm rested along the back, his hand moving gently on the nape of her neck. She felt a tremor of excitement.

'Come on, Fel, you know you've been on hot bricks all this time, terrified of doing something they'd disapprove of. As if you were a child, afraid to do anything Mummy might not like.' His smile teased her. 'Oh, it's not your fault—they've kept you on a pretty tight rein and even though you might seem to have your independence you've never had it completely, have you? But now they've admitted you're grown up and handed over responsibility to you. They've gone away—left the country for, what is it, two months?—and you've got to cope alone. Make your own decisions.' He shifted closer, his face close to hers, his mouth tantalising her lips. 'So what decisions are you going to make, Fenella?'

'Decisions?' she whispered. Her head was swimming. 'What—what about?'

'Why. . .' His lips were touching hers now, brushing them very gently before settling in for a long, lingering kiss '. . .about us, of course. . .'

She hadn't made the decision that night. Or perhaps she had. Perhaps she had made it all those weeks ago, when he had first walked into the library and she had seen him standing there in that shaft of sunlight. Whatever the truth might be, she moved into his cottage a week later. And, having once burned her boats, considered herself committed to him irrevocably.

Jenny could have told her she was being a fool. But Jenny wasn't there. She was away on a long course, and her place had been taken by a severe woman in her fifties who disapproved of talking in libraries and maintained a buttoned-up silence the whole time she was there.

In any case, Fenella thought later, it would have made no difference. Nothing anyone could have said would have made any difference.

Looking back at that period over a distance of years, she knew that her reaction had been extreme. Her upbringing had been an anachronism from which she'd never fully escaped. She was like a piece of elastic, stretched to its limit and then suddenly released. Jeremy had been no more than a catalyst, coming on the scene when she had been ready to snap. If he had not been there, something else would have happened.

He couldn't entirely be blamed. But at the time she didn't see it that way.

They had been together for six weeks when he came in one evening, dropped the newspaper on the table and said casually, 'That's it, then. I'm off in a couple of weeks.'

Fenella stared at him. 'Off? Off where?'

'Singapore,' he said, as if he were just going down the street. 'I've got a teaching job there. Great pay, house provided—servants—and a wonderful social life.' He gave her his charming smile. 'Pity you can't come along too, but I gather they've already got librarians.'

Fenella sat down suddenly, her legs shaking. 'Jeremy. . .you're joking.'

'No, I'm not. I heard this morning. Didn't expect to be going as quickly as this, I must admit, but apparently they've got a sudden crisis on, someone taken ill or died or something. So it's what my uncle in the Navy used to call a pierhead jump.' He came over to her, sat down beside her and slipped his arms round her shoulders. 'Don't look so shattered, Fel. I know it's a bit sudden—but we've had a good time together, haven't we? Had a lot of fun, laughs. And maybe you could come out to see me some time, once I know my way around. It'd be great to show you round Singapore.'

He was talking as if he were already there. Fenella searched for words, but how could she speak when her feelings were in such turmoil? When her heart was like a pool of molten lead, sinking down through her body, lying heavy in her stomach? When she felt sick and shaky, and as if the world were slipping away from her, roaring in her ears, black around her eyes. . .

'Here, don't go and faint on me.' Jeremy's voice came alarmed through the mist that threatened to engulf her. 'Fel. . . *Fel*. . .put your head down. Look, have a drink.' She felt him move away from her, then return and hold a glass to her lips. She sipped, felt her head clear a little, looked up at him and smiled tremulously. 'It can't be that much of a shock,' he said, and there was a slight note of injury in his voice. 'You knew I was only here for a term.'

Had she known that? Dimly, Fenella knew that she had. But she'd forgotten it, pushed the knowledge away. She hadn't wanted to know it, hadn't wanted to look ahead.

But now, slowly, horrifyingly, the truth was beginning to dawn.

'I'm sorry,' she said in a whisper. 'I've been feeling a bit off-colour all day.' It wasn't true, but she couldn't let Jeremy know that her weakness had been due to the blow he had just dealt her—the death-blow to all the hopes and dreams she had built up over the past weeks.

Instantly, he was all concern.

'Have you? Oh, you poor darling—and here am I, coming in full of my good news, not even noticing. Yes, you do look a bit wan.' He put his fingers under her chin, tipped her face up to examine it. 'What is it, flu?' A trace of alarm showed in his blue eyes. 'You don't think——?'

'No,' she reassured him at once, never even thinking that this might be a way to hold him. 'I'm not pregnant.' And, even if it had occurred to her, she thought later, she would never have used such a hold. And knew that she had a deep reservoir of pride, hitherto unsuspected, that had come to her rescue and saved her from the ultimate humiliation.

'Well, let's look after you, then. Let's get you to bed.' For a moment, a smile crinkled his face, and, for the first time, Fenella noticed that it didn't reach his eyes. Not entirely. But the charm of his handsome face, his white teeth, his boyish good looks, concealed that fact, as they had concealed it ever since she had known him.

All this time and she had never noticed.

All this time, and she'd been blind.

She was never conscious of having made a decision then. It was as if it was already made.

'No, thanks, Jeremy.' Her head clear now, she rose to her feet. 'I'm all right—really. And I'm going now, anyway.'

'Going?' he echoed. 'Going where?'

'Back to my flat.' She forced a smile. 'There's something I want to do there. . .and I may stay the night. In fact, I think it'll be just as well if I move back altogether, don't you?'

'Move back?' He stared at her, then gave a short laugh. 'Oh, I see! You're in a huff over Singapore. Look, Fel, I told you, I asked about you but there just isn't a job available at present. Anyway, I don't suppose you'd have wanted to come, would you?' He waited for a reply, and when she didn't speak, went on, hiding the uneasiness in his tone by beginning to bluster. 'Look, you never expected anything to come of our little fling, did you? I mean, surely that was understood from the start—that's all it was. You knew it wasn't meant to last—otherwise, why did you keep on your flat?'

It had been a shrewd blow. Fenella gazed at him, unable to answer. She'd kept her flat on because she hadn't wanted to move all her things to Jeremy's tiny, rented cottage. Because she knew that, once gone, it would be difficult to find another. Because. . .because she'd known this wasn't going to last?

Was it true?

She swayed again and put a hand to her head.

'I'm sorry, Jeremy. I can't argue about it now. I can't think. . . All I know is, I want to go back to my flat tonight. Tomorrow——'

'Tomorrow, you'll come waltzing back as if nothing had happened,' he said, his voice suddenly hard. 'And expect to take up where we left off. And try to trap me into—into some sort of commitment. Into marriage.' His eyes were glittering and she looked at him and wondered how she had ever found this handsome, charming man in any way attractive. 'Well, it won't work. No doubt I'll miss you—you've been a delightful companion these past weeks. Totally inexperienced, of course, but promising—yes, quite promising.' His teeth showed in a brief, cruel smile. 'Pity we haven't had time to bring you to your full potential. But some girls do need a lot more time than others, don't they?'

Fenella walked past him without a word. She went up to the bedroom and quickly gathered up the few things she would need for the night. She went down the stairs, out through the tiny hall and down the short garden path to her car.

She didn't say goodbye, and Jeremy did not emerge from the living-room to speak to her. She went back to her flat, spent a tearless night there and returned to the cottage next day, when she knew Jeremy would be at the college, to collect the rest of her belongings.

Two days later, she heard the news that both her parents had been killed in a road accident on the freeway near Toronto. She never saw Jeremy again.

CHAPTER EIGHT

'TIME went by in a blur for those first few months,' Fenella whispered against Robert's warm, naked shoulder. 'It was as if my whole world had fallen in. . . And there was so much to be done. I had to fly to Canada and arrange the funeral and cremation there. And there were all the formalities—with Mum and Dad not being Canadians. I needed papers. . . It was a nightmare.'

'And nobody to support you,' Robert murmured, holding her close. 'Deserted by the man you loved——'

'*Thought* I loved,' Fenella said quickly, and felt his arms tighten in loving gratitude. 'It wasn't real—none of what I had with Jeremy was real. But I didn't know that then. I never knew what love was until I met you.'

'I wish I'd known you then,' he said, and she sighed her agreement. But it wasn't until much later that she and Robert had met.

Once back in England, there had been so much to do, and Fenella had felt so alone. And her heart had been frozen, nothing more than an icicle throbbing coldly in her breast.

Once it's all over, she had thought, once everything's settled, I'll go away. There's nothing here for me now, after all. I'll make a new start, somewhere

I've never been before. Perhaps that will make me come back to life.

And she had tried. Putting most of the money she had inherited from her parents' modest savings and the sale of their house into investments, she had used the rest to take herself abroad. For a year, she had wandered around Europe, immersing herself in art galleries and museums, sitting at pavement cafés watching the world go by, teaching herself the languages she needed to know. She had fended off the advances of Italians and Frenchmen, parried the approaches of Germans and Dutch, shaken her head at Spaniards and Portuguese. She had been miserably lonely.

America had come next. It had taken courage to cross the Atlantic again, after her last journey there, but she had steered clear of Canada, much as she had always wanted to visit it, and headed instead for California and Arizona. Here she had visited San Francisco, Carmel, Yosemite and the Grand Canyon, and because she could not stay idle she had taken jobs wherever she went—as a waitress, as a shop assistant, doing anything and everything in an effort to beat off the unhappiness that still threatened to crowd in on her. In an effort to stave off the terrifying prospect of a life spent entirely alone.

Yet, lonely as she was, she had never been able to make a close friend. Always, the memory of Jeremy had haunted her, and she knew that she could never again risk such a cruel betrayal.

And, at last, she had come home. Knowing that if she was ever to find peace, it had to be in England. And that only by coming back to face the fears that haunted her mind would she ever be able to defeat them.

She had run for long enough.

The price of the London flat had shaken her, but the estate agent had assured her drily that it was as near a bargain as anyone could expect to find now in the teeming city, with the enormous pressures there were on accommodation. 'A lot of people take lodgers to help pay the mortgage,' he said helpfully. 'You've got two nice bedrooms here—someone would be glad to pay you at least fifty or sixty pounds a week for one of those.'

But Fenella shook her head. The thought of sharing her home with a stranger filled her with distaste. After more than two years spent travelling, she wanted nothing more than a place of her own, quiet and restful after a day spent out there in the jungle that London had become. She wanted no one else to destroy the peace that was so essential to her.

She walked to the window and looked out. The flat was in one of the gracious old houses that had once shared a railed and locked garden with its neighbours. The garden was still there, railed and leafy, but it was open to all now and girls from nearby offices were sitting on the grass, eating their lunchtime sandwiches and catching the unexpectedly mild winter sun before going back to their jobs, while old ladies and decrepit gentlemen sat on the seats, watching toddlers stagger along the narrow paths.

'I'll take it,' she said, looking around the high,

beautifully proportioned room, knowing suddenly that she could make this her home.

The young man looked a little startled. Evidently he was unused to buyers who made up their minds instantly. 'Er—you mean at the asking price?'

Fenella smiled. 'No.' Even she wasn't as naïve as that! She offered a figure that was below the asking price but still, she was sure, within the seller's margin, and he nodded, clearly more at ease now that she was behaving in the conventional manner.

'Right,' he said briskly, becoming businesslike. 'I'll get in touch with the vendor and put your offer to him, and then I'll come back to you. Er—will you be requiring finance? Would you like us to arrange that for you?'

Fenella smiled again. 'No finance needed, thank you.' It would drain her resources almost to nothing, but she would obviously not be able to find a flat in London for much less and it must be an investment. Prices were rising by the minute, the young man had told her as they came here. The money might as well be here as sitting in a bank somewhere.

That settled, she turned her attention to finding a job. She had been determined to make an entirely fresh start, rebuild her life, but she was equally determined that this time she would do nothing rash, nothing without deliberation.

After much thought, she went to the temping agency. She wasn't ready to commit herself yet, and she had gained enough experience now to be able to tackle almost any job. And, lonely though she continued to be, she was still wary of making close friends. Losing the first man she had ever loved, and then both parents, had made her ultra-cautious. She didn't want to risk that kind of pain again. . .ever.

Working as a temp would act as a shield against the danger of close relationships.

But not, as she was soon to discover, an impregnable shield.

She had been in the flat for just three weeks when Gina, from downstairs, invited her to a party.

'A party. . . I'm not sure.' Fenella was caught off guard, coming in from the shops with her arms full of shopping. She looked at the other girl, a wispy, fair-haired wraith who always reminded her of Edith Piaf and looked as if she might blow away with the first puff of wind.

'Oh, do come.' Gina's looks belied her; she was the mother of two lusty sons of four and six who filled the garden with their voices and played complicated games in the square every Saturday morning. 'It's to welcome my brother—he's been in Australia for four years and knows absolutely no one in London, and I'm asking everyone in the house. Please come. Besides, it's time we got to know you,' she added. 'You've been here nearly a month and I'm feeling guilty.'

Fenella laughed. 'All right—I'd love to come. When is it?'

'Tomorrow evening. Come about eight. It'll just be a dozen or so of us—everyone who lives here, and my brother and a friend he's brought with him. I'm doing a buffet meal, so don't eat too much beforehand—though, if there's anything left, my two monsters will make short work of it the next day.' She wrinkled her small nose and disappeared into her own flat, leaving Fenella to continue up the stairs feeling slightly uneasy, as if she had just committed herself to something she wasn't at all sure of.

But that was nonsense, she told herself. It was a party, that was all. She didn't even have to stay late if she didn't want to. She could just appear and then, after a suitable length of time, make some excuses and leave.

So why did she have this feeling that her life, which she had so carefully organised, was about to be turned upside-down—yet again?

'And this is our new neighbour, Fenella Sutcliffe.' Gina touched Fenella's arm, turning her to face a tall, bronzed man with hair as black as her own and eyes only a slightly darker shade of grey. 'Fenella, this is Mike's friend, Robert Milburn. Professor Robert Milburn, I should say.'

'Indeed you shouldn't. This is a party, not an official presentation.' His voice was deep and pleasant, without a trace of the Australian accent she had expected. Seeing the expression on her face, he laughed. 'I'm not from Oz—Mike just picked me up there. Actually, I'm a historian. I went Down Under to do some research and we met there and met up again in London.' His grey eyes settled on her face. 'How about you?'

'Me?' Fenella looked at him blankly. She was experiencing the oddest sensation, somewhere in the region of her heart. A quivering, kicking motion that seemed vaguely familiar. . .and then she knew what it was. The sensation she'd felt when she'd first

met Jeremy. Only this time it was about ten times
more powerful.

Oh, no, she thought. Not again. Not when I
thought I'd got my life settled at last. . .

Robert Milburn was watching her. His eyes
seemed darker, the pupils wider. Her heart thudded
again. She looked for a way of escape, but there was
none.

'Yes. Recent life history, you know. Gina said you
were a new neighbour. I take it that means you've
just moved into a flat here.'

'That's right. The one above this.'

He grinned. 'I should think that's better than
being in the one below—with Gina's fairy-footed
pair stamping about overhead. Apparently the old
couple who have the basement flat are deaf, but
whether they acquired that desirable state after Gina
moved in I haven't been able to ascertain.'

Fenella managed a laugh. 'I think they're rather
fun. Gina's boys, I mean, not the couple in the
basement.'

'In small doses. So. . .where did you live before
you came here?'

'Oh, nowhere in particular.' She saw his thick
black eyebrows go up and added hastily, 'I don't
mean I was of no fixed abode—although I suppose
that's just what I was, really. I've been abroad for
the past two or three years.'

'Sounds interesting,' he commented, but Fenella
shook her head. She was beginning to feel more in
command of herself, but it was an effort and she
wasn't sure just how long she would be able to keep
it up. If only there were some way out of this, some

way she could escape from this man, but they were in a corner and the only door was a french window—she could hardly rush out into the night. She took a deep breath, trying to overcome the rising panic within her.

'Not really. I wasn't doing anything in particular. I looked at art galleries and museums and things in Europe and then went to America for a while.'

'You make it sound as if you'd just done a couple of rather boring shopping trips. There must have been more to it than that.'

Fenella met his eyes, meaning to deny it, but the expression in them caught her off balance and she hesitated, started to say something, stopped and floundered. To her astonished dismay, her eyes were suddenly brimming with tears and Robert Milburn's face was filled with concern. He reached out and put a hand under her elbow as she swayed towards him.

'Fenella, are you all right? Look—we'll go through here.' He led her swiftly out through the french windows into Gina's garden. It was cool and quiet, the sounds of the party flooding out into the wintry night. She took a few deep breaths, swallowed once or twice and then faced him with as brilliant a smile as she could muster.

'Thank you. I'm quite all right now. I just felt rather hot suddenly.'

But his eyes were on her face and she knew that he didn't believe her.

'Something upset you,' he said quietly. 'Something I said—or something you said yourself, perhaps. What was it, Fenella? Do you think you could tell me?'

She shook her head, and her eyes filled again. Damn—what was the matter with her? After all these years of keeping emotion at bay, not allowing tears to overwhelm her, why should she suddenly feel like weeping her heart out, just because a pair of grey eyes had looked into hers and a warm, deep voice had spoken and touched the strings of her heart. . .? She put a shaking hand up to her face and found her fingers clasped in Robert Milburn's. Trembling, she stood helpless, her eyes raised to his, not knowing that in her expression was all the pain and yearning she had kept repressed for so long; not knowing that at that moment she was a living epitome of all the grief and loss that had been suffered by humanity throughout existence.

Robert Milburn's eyes narrowed. He released her fingers and slid his hand along her arm. With a swift movement, he drew her against him and held her there, warm and steady, so that she could feel the drumbeat of his heart.

'I'm going to take you back to your flat, Fenella,' he said quietly. 'Don't worry about Gina—I'll think of something to tell her. And then, one day soon, we're going to meet again and talk. We have a lot to talk about, you and I. I think you know it, don't you?'

She looked up at him and felt her heart tremble. But there was nothing she could say, no denial she could make. And as she let him lead her through the garden to the main door of the house, she knew that this meeting had been inevitable. And that the rest of her life was, indeed, about to begin.

* * *

There was really very little she could do about it after that. It was, in some ways, uncannily similar to that other 'first' meeting with Robert, at the hospital. The look in his dark grey eyes. The sensation of drowning, the feeling that life had caught her up in its jaws, was carrying her off and did not mean to let her go. The sense of inevitability, of helplessness. . .

On that first night, when Robert had taken her back to her flat, she had been tense, expecting him to want to stay. How she would have reacted to such a suggestion she never really knew—the inexplicable fear that filled her at the thought was tangled with a burning excitement that set her heart leaping.

But Robert didn't suggest staying. He saw her into her living-room, giving an approving glance at the pale silvery-green walls and off-white carpet, and made her sit on the big couch which had been her most extravagant buy. Then he stood for a moment, looking at her with grave eyes.

'You look pale,' he said abruptly. 'I'm going to make you a drink. What would you like?'

'Oh, no, please, there's no need——' she began, but he silenced her with a flick of his fingers. 'Well— what I'd like more than anything else is a cup of tea. But I can make it myself—I'm quite all——'

He strode across the room, ignoring her. 'Is this the kitchen? I thought so. No—don't move. I'm quite capable of finding a kettle.' His voice came through the open door. 'You've got two kinds of tea here—Darjeeling and Earl Grey. I'm making Earl Grey, is that all right?' She heard the sounds of the kettle being filled and cups found and set on saucers. 'You don't take sugar, do you? I thought not. You don't mind if I have a cup too, I hope?' He came through the door with a tray in his hands. 'To tell you the truth, Gina's punch was beginning to turn a bit sour on me. I don't really like to drink a lot of alcohol.'

Fenella watched him as he set the tray on a low table. He poured two cups, handed one to her and then settled himself in the armchair opposite. She thought again of Jeremy, who would certainly have chosen the couch, sitting beside her and taking the opportunity to inch closer.

And at the same time she felt a twinge of what in any other circumstances she would have recognised as disappointment.

'Do you care to talk to me about whatever upset you?' he asked after a moment, his tone casual. 'Was it something I said?'

Fenella shook her head. Nothing he had said—just the way he had looked. The way he had looked at *her*. The sudden feeling that she had had, that everything was happening too late—that they ought to have met years ago. Before Jeremy. Before she had closed her heart forever.

'No. It was nothing. Just a—a silly moment. Probably because I'm rather tired,' she said, and smiled as brightly as she knew how, to prove that there was nothing wrong.

The expression in Robert's eyes changed and she turned quickly away. For a moment, she could have sworn that they held tenderness—but that was ridiculous. They had only just met—how could he possibly feel anything towards her other than a polite interest?

'Very well,' he said after a moment, and she wanted to weep again at the gentleness in his voice. 'I won't pester you any more now. But one day, I hope you'll trust me enough to tell me. . . We are going to meet again, aren't we?'

'Are we?' she whispered, not daring to look at him.

'Yes.' It was a statement, firmly made in that deep, positive voice. 'And we're going to make it soon. Tomorrow—no, damn it, I've got an appointment in Portsmouth I can't get out of, won't be back till late. . . The next day, then. Are you free for dinner?' He waited while Fenella fought to control her skidding heart, then added, 'Please?'

It was that 'please' that proved to be her undoing. It was almost as if *he* were anxious—as if he thought she might refuse. In that moment, she knew that it just wasn't in her to refuse anything this man asked—and even though the warning bells were jangling in her mind, even though she knew that this could be her most dangerous adventure yet, there was no question, somehow, of her saying 'no'.

It needn't go any further, she told herself. Just one dinner. . .what harm can that do? Just one evening in a lifetime . . .

But even then she knew that it wouldn't stop there.

She went through her work that day in a haze, returning to the flat to stare at her wardrobe and wonder what to wear. Eventually, with seven-thirty looming closer, she pulled out a plain suit in silky turquoise jersey. The fine fabric clung to the slender curves of her body and the colour contrasted vividly with her dark hair, throwing glints of sea-green into her eyes. But Fenella, leaning forward to peer into the mirror as her trembling fingers applied lipstick and eye make-up, was aware of none of these things. She saw only worry in the wide eyes and a pallor in her cheeks that she did her best to correct with blusher.

Whatever happened, she wasn't going to let Robert Milburn know just how ridiculously scared she felt at the thought of spending an evening with him.

When he arrived, punctual to the minute, she looked as cool and poised as any girl who was accustomed to being wined and dined by attractive men. The silk jersey swished against her legs as she let him in, and she caught his glance resting approvingly on her figure. Quelling the immediate disturbance this set up inside her, and concentrating on the inevitable pleasure of knowing she looked attractive, she took the flowers he handed her and thanked him.

'They're beautiful. Freesias are my favourites— they're so delicate, and the scent's lovely. I'll put them in water straight away—do help yourself to a drink.'

She went into the kitchen for a vase and came back to find him pouring a glass of lemonade.

'Don't you want anything stronger?'

He shook his head. 'Not at the moment, thanks. We'll be having wine with the meal and I have to drive.' His eyes studied her, grey as satin-polished steel. 'You're looking better this evening.'

'Thank you.' She arranged the flowers, aware that her colour had risen almost as much as if he had paid her an extravagant compliment. 'Actually, there was nothing wrong with me—I was just a little tired. I popped in to apologise to Gina and thank her for the party and she said it had broken up quite early anyway.'

'I don't know,' he said. 'I didn't go back.'

There was a short silence. Fenella set the vase on a small table. She glanced sideways at Robert and, seeing that his gaze was fixed abstractedly on the picture that hung over the fireplace, allowed herself to observe him more directly.

He really was quite impressive—broad shoulders to go with that height, tapering away to a narrow waist and hips, with long legs that would, she thought, have looked their best in sleek Regency-style leather boots, fitted exactly to the calves. But Robert Milburn, she suspected, would not have enjoyed the Regency period at all—he was too restlessly vibrant, the energy crackling from him, to have fitted in as a court dandy. He didn't even look like the academic that, as a professor of history, he must be—he looked more like an adventurer, an explorer, a true man of action.

Even tonight, immaculately sophisticated in his silver-grey suit with matching tie and discreet gold cufflinks and watch, he looked as if he would be equally at home in a ski-suit or wrapped in the protective, padded gear of a daredevil parachutist.

He turned his head suddenly, catching Fenella's gaze on him. As his eyes met hers, she gave a tiny gasp. She wanted to look away, but couldn't; their glances held and she felt the colour warm her cheeks again as her heart flung itself against her ribs as if in a frantic bid for freedom. Something deep inside her stomach twisted, and the heat spread across her abdomen, into her thighs. . . Unable to bear it, she moved quickly, closing a window, putting a book on a shelf, looking round for her handbag.

'Would. . .would you like any more to drink?' she asked, and heard her voice croak like that of a husky raven. She bit her lip and cursed her treacherous body. Why *did* he have to affect her like this?

'No, thanks. If you're ready, we'll be going.' He stood aside to allow her to precede him out of the door and she walked past him, shivering at his nearness in the doorway, aware that his eyes were on her, bright and ironic. Just let me get through this evening, she prayed. Just let me get through it without making a fool of myself. . . I'll never ask for anything again, never.

His car was at the door, a sleek grey Jaguar, and he opened the passenger door and handed her into it as if she were a princess. In spite of herself, Fenella felt herself thaw a little. Jeremy, of course, would have done the same thing—but there had been a brittle shallowness about his good manners, as if they had been taken from a cupboard and dusted off for the occasion. With Robert Milburn, they seemed natural—as if he had been born with them, grown up with them.

As if they stemmed from a natural courtesy and consideration, rather than a book of etiquette, or cool calculation.

He took her to a restaurant near Covent Garden,

parking near the Opera House and then leading her into one of the side-streets. There was nothing to show, on the outside, that there was any restaurant there—simply the blank brick wall of a long build-ing, with a few small doors that suggested trades-men's entrances. Perhaps most were—but at one of them Robert stopped and led her through and down some stairs into a basement.

Fenella peered into the dimness. She could see that there was a bar, with a dining area close by, with further tables through a series of brick arches. As her eyes grew accustomed to the low light, she saw that each table was lit by a single fat candle, and that the walls were covered with photographs.

'Actors, mostly,' Robert told her as they were led to a table and given large menus. 'This place is very popular with theatricals, writers, TV people and so on. You never know whom you might see down here.'

Fenella glanced round, but could recognise no one. But then she hadn't had much time either to visit theatres or watch much TV in the past few years. She turned her attention to her menu instead.

'Mmm. . .it looks interesting. Black bean soup—stilton and walnut salad—garlic mushrooms—and that's only the starters!' She looked across the table at Robert and smiled suddenly, feeling unexpectedly at ease. 'Thank you for bringing me here.'

'I thought you might enjoy it,' he said quietly. 'It's informal, relaxed. I didn't want to come anywhere grand—not the first time. We'll save that for later.'

'Later?' Her heart skipped.

'Next time, or maybe the time after that.' His eyes

met hers. 'There are going to be other times, aren't there, Fenella?'

'If—if you want there to be,' she stammered. 'But we hardly know each other——'

'And that's just why we need to meet. To get to know each other.' He reached across the table and took her hand. 'Fenella, I'm not a philanderer. I've had my relationships—it would be odd if I hadn't, at my age. But I've never played with any woman, and I've never let anyone down. I don't intend to start now.' He waited a moment. 'Does that make you feel any happier?'

'I don't know what——'

'Don't say you don't know what I mean,' he cut in, sounding almost angry. 'Don't let's have any pretences between us, Fenella. I know you're as scared as a kitten of me—but I promise you I'm not some great fierce wolf, waiting to bite you in two. Nor am I going to end this evening by asking "my place or yours?" and expecting to go to bed.' He ignored the flare of colour in her cheeks. 'I simply want us to take our time in getting to know each other. That is,' he added, almost under his breath, 'if we can. . .'

Fenella did not ask him again what he meant. She knew, only too well.

The crackling electricity between herself and Robert Milburn was so vividly incandescent that she wondered that the other diners were not scorched by it. And she knew, as she sat there and felt her fingers tremble beneath his, that the attraction between them was too powerful to deny.

They might well try to slow it down, to get to

know each other as people before the clamour of
their bodies took control. But whether they would
succeed or not was another question. And as she sat
there, staring unseeingly at the menu, her body
quivered again with panic—and with a deep and
overruling desire.

CHAPTER NINE

SLOWLY, slowly, Fenella learned to trust Robert Milburn. He treated her with a quiet, gentle insistence that refused to allow her to withdraw from him as sometimes, in panic, she fought to do. At the same time, he gave her space; she never felt pressured, never trapped, and knew always that if she really wanted to escape him he would let her fly free.

But she didn't want to. As the weeks slipped by, with Fenella moving from office to office in her temping, Robert became the constant in her life, the factor that was always present, a beacon in the loneliness that she was only now beginning fully to realise. Ever since Jeremy, she had closed her heart to any form of relationship, and with the death of her parents she had become numb.

Slowly, surely, Robert Milburn was waking her from a long sleep.

Together, they went to theatres and concerts, to museums and art galleries. They took a boat trip to Hampton Court and lost themselves in the maze; they took another to Greenwich and marvelled at the observatory. They walked in the wind on Hampstead Heath and under the trees of Epping Forest; they explored Windsor, strolled by the river and admired the castle.

They talked for hours. About the books they read,

the films they'd seen, the music they liked. They found that their tastes didn't always coincide, and that they could sometimes get quite heated about an exchange of views, but the heat invariably evaporated in laughter. And there were enough similarities for a deep pleasure to grow between them when they heard an old Cole Porter song or watched a painfully romantic film on TV.

And they told each other about their lives. About their childhoods, their families, their friends. Robert told Fenella about the family home in the Cotswolds which he had inherited on the death of his father two or three years before, and where he planned to go to write his next book.

And, after a while, Fenella felt secure enough to tell him about Jeremy.

'I wonder now what I ever saw in him,' she said honestly. 'He was good-looking, charming, attentive—and I was so naïve, I just couldn't see past the surface gloss to the empty shell beneath. It never occurred to me that he was just using me to fill in time—a pleasant diversion while he waited for the next step up in his career.' She looked down, feeling the heat in her cheeks as she made the admission. 'I believed it was all for real—I was such a fool.'

'But very young,' Robert said quietly, and reached out to touch her hand where it lay on the table between them. 'And we all make our mistakes.'

Something in his voice made her look at him. 'You too?'

He nodded. 'None of us is invulnerable, Fenella. Yes, I've had my rough moments too. Only mine actually did lead to marriage. It's all right. . .' He

tightened his fingers on hers as she moved in alarm.
'It's all over now. It's been over for years.'

He was silent for a moment, his eyes hooded,
looking back into the past. Fenella waited, her eyes
on the fingers that were now intertwined on the
table. The restaurant was quiet, almost deserted;
most people had finished their meal and gone. Their
waiter had furnished them with coffee and liqueurs,
and disappeared.

'We were young too,' he said at last. 'Far too
young, far too headstrong—and far too much in
love. It was doomed from the start, but we couldn't
see it, of course. Do you know, I think one of the
most disastrous things that's happened in the past
few decades is the lowering of the age of majority to
eighteen. That's how old we were—eighteen.
Nobody could stop us doing whatever we wanted—
so we got married.'

'At eighteen?' Fenella said, and he nodded.

'We'd just started at university together. It was
crazy, of course. Everyone warned us against it. But
we were too dazzled by each other to listen.'

'So. . .what happened?'

'What do you think? Within a year, the cracks
were showing, within eighteen months they were too
wide and deep to mend. Helen met someone else
and moved in with him, and that was the end of it.
Fortunately, we were able to get divorced quietly
under what were then the new laws, and we parted
without too much bitterness and went on our way
sadder but wiser. At least,' he added, 'I was wiser—
Helen married twice after that and may be married
again for all I know. I haven't heard from her in

years. But I was like you—I steered clear for a long time.' He looked at her. 'I won't pretend that there's been no one since then, Fenella,' he said quietly. 'But there's never been anyone really important. Do you understand me?'

He had lifted his hand from hers and his fingertips were just touching the back of her hand. He moved them, slowly, sensuously, against her skin, barely brushing the tiny hairs that stood up to reach him. Fenella felt a shiver run through her whole body. She sat quite still, aware of nothing but his slowly moving fingers, of their delicate touch, of the electricity that tingled from them and through her palms, up the sensitive nerves of her inner arm and into her breasts. It was as if he were caressing her entire body, a distillation of erotic power that expressed itself in the minute touch of fingertip against skin.

'Do you understand?' he murmured again, and she lifted her eyes with an effort and found his gaze fixed on her, silver-bright, as penetrating as a sword. Immediately, she wanted to drop her own glance, but she was helpless, impelled. She parted her lips to speak, brushed them with her tongue and whispered, 'Yes. . .yes, I think I understand.'

He stared at her for a moment, and his eyes were dark now, the irises a shimmering rim of silver around the wide black pupils. His fingers trembled against hers, and Fenella felt her skin shiver in response. Her breath was coming quickly and there was a singing in her ears, as if waves were breaking on some wild and lonely shore.

'Let's go,' Robert said abruptly, and tugged her to her feet.

* * *

He took her home, his Jaguar moving like a shadow through almost deserted streets. The flats were in darkness when they arrived and Fenella unlocked her door quietly, though she knew that it was unlikely that they would disturb anyone. Gina and her husband and sons had moved away, to a house in the country, and the new occupants of their flat had not yet moved in. And the couple in the basement, deaf as they were, never heard a sound.

Inside, she moved to the tall lamp and switched it on. She felt Robert close behind her and turned into his arms. Her body was trembling.

'It's all right, my love,' he said quietly, holding her against him. 'It's all right. Just let's stand here together for a moment. . .quite still.'

Fenella put her hands on his arms and looked up into his face. His eyes were still dark, his mouth firm, a lock of black hair fell over his forehead and Fenella put up a shaky hand to brush it back. At once, he caught her wrist in his fingers and drew her hand against his lips. He kissed each finger in turn, laid his mouth against the back of her hand and then spread the fingers wide to sprinkle tiny, burning kisses in her palm and between each knuckle. As his lips touched the sensitive pulse on the inside of her wrist, he pulled her harder against him, and Fenella knew that he was as aroused as she. Her body shuddered with desire and longing, and Robert took his mouth from her hand and looked into her eyes.

'Fenella,' he muttered, and released her hand. He spread his fingers behind her head, tangling them in her short brown hair, and bent his head to hers. Almost without knowing it, she parted her lips and felt him touch them, gently, firmly, tenderly with his. With increasing pressure, he opened her mouth and she felt his tongue move, touching hers with an exquisite delicacy, as fine as the touch of a sharply honed blade. A flare of heat ran through her and she gasped, feeling his mouth move against hers, shaping it to his will. For a panic-stricken moment, she wanted to escape, tried to withdraw, but his mouth firmed on hers and she knew that she wanted no escape. Her arms slid up to encircle his neck; she pressed herself against him, feeling her soft curves blend with the hardness of his muscles, and let her tongue move against his, exploring the moist warmth of his mouth as he explored hers, lifting her face and arching her neck as his lips left hers and travelled down to find the wildly fluttering pulse in the hollow of her throat.

'Fenella,' he murmured, his voice deep and husky in his throat, 'do you have any idea what you're doing to me?'

Bemused, she shook her head. Her head was filled with the singing thunder of her heartbeat. Her skin burned and shivered, a thousand minute tingles quivering across a surface that was as acutely aware of his nearness as a butterfly was aware of nectar.

'Fenella,' he said, and put two fingers under her chin to tip her face up to his, 'we have to talk. We've circled around this for long enough. We've a lot to say to one another—we've known it from the beginning.' He paused and took a deep breath. 'And, until we do, I'm going to call a halt.'

She gave a little gasp, dismayed and imploring, knowing that she didn't want to stop now, that she wanted him to go on, to kiss her again, to touch her and hold her. The thought brought another flutter of panic to her throat, but her excitement overrode her fear. She knew only that with this man she could reach heights of rapturous sensation that she had never known, never even suspected with Jeremy. She knew that this was her man.

'Robert. . .' She whispered pleadingly, and he lifted her face and kissed her again, quietly this time, with no more than the lightest of pressure. 'Robert. . .'

'Not now, my sweet,' he said quietly. 'This is too important to rush. Don't worry—I'm not going to change my mind. But I want you to have time to change yours, if you want to.' His voice shook suddenly. 'I hope to heaven you don't want to. . . But you need this time, Fenella. Believe me, you need it.'

She looked up at him, feeling the tumult slowly calm in her body. His eyes were on hers, willing her to understand. Slowly, she nodded, knowing he was right. The course their story would take was inevitable, but to rush through the pages would be a mistake. Dimly, she remembered a Frank Sinatra song which said something about making all the stops along the way. And knew that Robert understood exactly.

'I'm going to leave you now,' he said softly. 'And I can't see you tomorrow. But the next evening—I'll call for you, at the usual time. We'll eat somewhere really special. And then. . .we'll talk.'

* * *

There had been no hint, Fenella thought when her memories brought her this far months later, that a day which began with such promise was to end in horror. Even now, close in Robert's arms again with months of blankness behind her, she found it difficult to let her mind stretch back past its self-imposed barrier to see just what had happened. But the knowledge of it was there, no longer to be escaped, and she knew that she must live it again, in all its appalling detail. Only then would it be exorcised from her mind; only then could she go freely into the rest of her life.

It had been a bright, warm day. In the square opposite her window, trees were laden with blossom, and daffodils fluttered myriad yellow flags in response from every window-box. Fenella had risen early, her heart already beating fast in anticipation, and looked out on a world that seemed to be holding its breath. For a few moments, everything was still under the tender blue spring sky, as if waiting for the fulfilment of a promise made long, long ago.

Robert had said, 'We'll talk'. But Fenella knew that it would not stop with talking. Tonight, his kisses would take her further than she had ever been before. Tonight, she would step beyond Jeremy, beyond the years of numbness, and learn to fly, for Robert would take her to the stars and there would be no limit.

She was thankful to have a busy day ahead of her in the office where she had only just begun to work, although it was not always easy to keep her mind on the routine and she couldn't help the occasional glance at her watch. But at last it was five o'clock

and she was free to go, smiling a goodbye at the
other girls and slipping away quickly so as to get
back to her flat, shower and change into the new
dress she had bought yesterday.

It was a sheath of pale, softly glowing amethyst,
its colour delicately startling against her pale skin
and dark brown hair. Fitting the slender lines of her
body exactly, it accentuated every gentle curve and
the colour blended perfectly with the silver of her
bracelet and earrings and the chain she hung around
her neck.

Fenella fastened the bracelet and looked into the
mirror. Her eyes were huge, almost frightened. But
there was nothing to fear, she told herself. This was
Robert, who had been so gentle, so patient. Robert:
the man she loved. The man she would always love.

And as the doorbell gave a short, quick ring, her
heart leapt. He was here. The evening had begun.

The 'somewhere special' turned out to be a restaurant of discreet, dimly lit luxury where Robert
had booked a corner table beside a tall potted palm,
and where the waiters, having served them, with-
drew to reappear magically only when required.

Fenella could never remember just what she
ordered that evening. Something to do with salmon,
she thought, for her main course—and had it been a
soufflé, light as a bubble, for starters? As for dessert,
she probably hadn't had any at all; perhaps a scrap
of cheese from Robert's plate. But whatever she had
eaten it had been delicious, she knew that—she
remembered saying so. And the wine had matched
it perfectly, leaving her in a state of pleasurable

relaxation and a haze of love for the man who sat so close.

'Have you been thinking over the past two days?' he asked as they sipped their coffee. 'I've thought of nothing else.' His eyes held hers. 'You know what I want to ask you, don't you?' he said quietly.

Fenella dropped her gaze for a moment. Now that the moment had come, she was almost afraid to go ahead. If only time would stop now, she thought as her heart kicked inside her. If only we could keep it here, with Robert looking at me like that, with the edge of his little finger just barely moving against mine, and with all the yearning over and the joy yet to begin. . . Once she had given her answer, everything would be different, changed. And, although she wanted the change, wanted it desperately, she couldn't help wanting to hold it away from her for a brief space longer, for the sensation of a suspense that would never come again.

'Fenella?' he said, and she knew from the suppressed tension in his voice that she must delay no longer.

'Yes, Robert,' she said softly, and raised her eyes to meet his. 'I know.'

The finger that was touching hers made a quick, spasmodic movement and she turned her hand to meet his, feeling the quick, strong beat of his pulse against hers. Palm to palm, their hands stretched together, the fingers extending their length in quivering contact before twining around each other in close surrender. Fenella felt her heart skip. A sensation of warmth, almost fluid, spread from deep within her, flooding through her body, down her

arms to the fingertips that Robert held in his, down
her legs to toes that curled inside her sandals. She
gazed into Robert's eyes and knew that there was no
one else in the world at that moment; that the world
was theirs, narrowed down to a table in a tiny, dim
alcove and surrounded by tall green plants.

'Please, Robert,' she said on a breath, 'take me
home.'

They hadn't turned on the light that time. The moon
had come shining through the windows to illuminate
the room, turning it into a magical place of silver
and shadow. And they had not lingered in the living-
room. With one quick, decisive movement, Fenella
had led Robert straight through to the bedroom,
where the moonlight had lain like a glimmering silk
coverlet across the wide bed.

It was almost, she thought now, her memories
drawing her ever closer to that final horrific moment,
as if it had been a rehearsal for this night. A subtle,
tender   foreshadowing   of   what   was   to
come. . .except that as they had stood by the bed,
their bodies close and warm, there had been no hint
at all of what was to come; no intimation that this
night was to be wiped from her mind for many
months, together with everything that had happened
before. She trembled in Robert's arms, wanting even
now to blot out that last terrible picture, and he held
her close, murmuring in her ear.

'It's all right, darling. It's all over. It's not going
to happen again. Let your mind go—let yourself
remember it. It's better that you do—now. You
have to face it.'

'I know,' she whispered, and felt a rush of gratitude for his understanding. But it was his memory too, wasn't it? He'd suffered as well on that last evening. He'd suffered as much as she had—more.

She remembered the sensitivity he'd displayed even then. His concern for her on that evening when everything had seemed so simple, before disaster had broken in.

'Fenella. . .you're sure about this? I don't want——'

'I'm sure,' she'd whispered against his breast.

'I'm asking you to marry me. Not just sleep with me. You do understand that?'

'Oh, Robert.' She reached up to draw his face down to hers. 'I'll marry you tomorrow if you like. But please, let's have tonight first. . . I want you so much.'

She felt him smile against her cheek, and her heart leapt as he drew her closer, pressing her firmly against him.

'You're a brazen hussy, you know that? But I love you. . .oh, lord how I love you. . .' And there was a sudden rough passion in his voice, an almost desperate need of her that ground out of him as if it had been suppressed for too long, as if he had been waiting for this moment, needing it, from the very first time they had met. And as she met his lips with a joyous abandon that took her completely by surprise, Fenella knew that he had—and that she had been waiting too. For so long. . .for all her life. And had never known it.

With a deep groan, Robert picked her up and carried her to the bed. He laid her down with a gentleness that seemed to match the soft glow of the moonlight that washed over her, and then reached down to unfasten the tiny buttons that ran down the length of her amethyst dress. With sensuous fingers, the tips just brushing the silk of her skin, he drew it aside to reveal her slender body, covered now by only a brief, lacy bra and pants. He knelt beside the bed, his hands caressing her breasts as he removed the bra, and then he laid his cheek on them, his lips touching her nipples, teasing them into erection while his hand slipped down over her waist and hip to slide the last flimsy covering away from her body, fingertips roaming with almost casual nonchalance as he did so, stroking her from thigh to instep.

Fenella lay still, shivering under his delicate touch. Her eyes closed, emotions reeling, she was barely aware of what he was doing, and then she felt him close beside her on the bed. As his skin touched hers, she gasped and knew that he had felt the same shock of delight at the contact of their nakedness.

She turned her face to his and felt his lips on her mouth, opening and shaping it as he had done before, his tongue making a tender inroad, exploring her moistness, developing a pulsating rhythm of its own that had her gasping and twisting in his arms. She could feel his length stretched against hers, the rough friction of his body hair against her own smooth skin, the taut strength of his muscles against her melting softness. And, as she shifted against him, wanting to come even closer, she felt the heat of desire sweep over her like the waters of a breaking dam, urgent, overwhelming, totally unstoppable.

'Robert. . .' She whispered against his mouth. 'Robert. . .please. . .oh, Robert, I love you.'

'I love you too,' he muttered, and a groan tore from his throat. 'Fenella—oh, Fenella. . .'

She twisted beneath him, drawing him tight against her, knowing that in the next moment they would be together, as close as it was possible for two human beings to be; welcoming it, needing it, demanding it. . .

And then, harshly, unbelievably, there was a crash from the other room. The sudden, horrific sound of splintering glass. An exclamation. An oath. A laugh. . .

Fenella felt Robert's movements cease abruptly. Her own body was rigid with bewilderment and sudden flaring terror. She felt a rush of cold air as he lifted himself away from her, and turned her head to see him reaching for his clothes.

'What the hell——?'

There was a sudden silence from the other room. Fenella, trembling with fear on the bed, heard a murmur of voices. Robert was dragging his trousers up to his waist, fumbling with the fastening, already halfway across the room, but before he could reach the door it was kicked open and swung violently towards him. Fenella looked past him and gave a cry of terror.

The bulk of the man filled the doorway, exaggerated by the moonlight to a horrifying proportion. Huge, black and menacing, he stood quite still for a moment, only the shine of his eyes betraying any movement as he stared at the scene before him. Then Robert lunged towards him; he reacted swiftly, with violence, and the room was suddenly filled with noise, with black shapes that struggled and swayed, kicked and punched, grunted and cursed and swore. Fenella crouched on the bed, watching with dilated eyes. There were at least three of them, three men attacking Robert, three men who seemed intent on killing him. She could only crouch there doing nothing.

Reaching beside her for the table lamp, she pulled the plug from its socket and swung the heavy base in the air. As the biggest of the men rolled near her, she brought it down hard, and felt it make sickening contact.

The man swore loudly in pain. He scrambled up and she saw him loom over her in the moonlight. Teeth and eyes flashed as he reached out and caught her roughly by the shoulder.

'You little bitch!' His voice was a snarl. 'Here— let's have some light—see just what we've got here.'

One of the men found the switch and snapped on the light. Fenella flinched at the sudden brightness and then looked frantically for Robert.

He was lying on the floor, with the third man on top of him. Blood was oozing from a cut on his head, and he looked as if he was unconscious.

'It's all right,' the biggest man said with a sneer. 'Your boyfriend's all right. So far.' His hot eyes moved over Fenella's naked, shivering body. 'Doing all right, was he?' he asked insinuatingly.

'Please,' Fenella said in a shaking voice, 'please, take whatever you want and go away.'

'And have you ring the police the minute we're out of the door? No, I don't reckon so—not for a while, anyway.' He grinned round at his fellows. 'Didn't expect to find the lady in, did we? But now we have—well, we might as well have our bit of fun. Don't see why matey here should get it all, do you?'

Fenella saw the grins on their faces and felt the fear creep over her. Frantically, she scrabbled further back on the bed. 'No—no, please. . .' But she knew that her fear was exciting them more; she could see their expressions, lascivious and obscene, as they moved in closer.

Desperately, she looked for help to Robert, still lying on the floor. But although his eyes were open now and he was clearly as frantic as she, he did not move. And, as the shadows closed over her, she knew that he could not.

And then the memories stopped.

CHAPTER TEN

WHIMPERING, shuddering, as terrified as she had been on that night, Fenella turned in Robert's arms and buried her face against his bare shoulder. She could feel him holding her close, his body warm and strong against hers, his heart beating strongly against her breast. For a long time, she clung to him, then, slowly, her rigid body relaxed and her trembling ceased. She lay still, breathing more regularly, facing her memories at last.

'What happened?' she asked at last in a low voice. 'What—what did they do to us? I can only remember looking at you on the floor and knowing you couldn't help me—after that, there's nothing.' She shuddered. 'I don't think I'll ever want to remember what happened next—but I need to know.'

'I hope you never do remember it,' he said soberly. 'There have been times—a thousand times—when I've wished I could forget too. Lying on that floor, helpless, having to watch. . . Fenella, that's a hell I never want to go through again. They'd kicked me so hard they'd damaged my spine—I was paralysed from the waist down. But once they realised I couldn't do anything they ignored me. And while they were. . .turning their attention to you, I managed to drag myself to the phone. I dialled 999 and gave the number before they realised what I was doing, and then of course they came for me again.

But I was glad enough of that—at least it took them away from you. And the operator could hear enough of what was going on to know that we needed help, fast. The police were there in minutes.'

Fenella held him tightly, trying to imagine what it must have been like for him, having to watch, knowing he was helpless. Yet he'd still managed to summon help. . . 'They might have killed you,' she said with a shiver. 'They might have killed us both.' Then, after a moment's hesitation, because she had to know, she asked, 'Did they—when they'd decided you couldn't help me any more, did they——?'

'They didn't get as far as rape, no,' he said quietly. 'Thank heaven, I managed to distract them from that. Though it was certainly what they meant to do.' His hands were firm and reassuring on her body. 'They barely had a chance to touch you, my darling,' he said softly. 'I promise you that.'

Fenella relaxed again. The thought of those unknown men, forcing their brutal bodies on hers with Robert helpless to do anything about it, filled her with repugnance. She felt again a shadow of the terror she had felt that night and knew why her mind had blocked out the memory. It had been too horrifying to face. Only when she had found herself in Robert's arms again, once more about to embark on the greatest adventure of her life, had it returned. . .as if her consciousness had been aware that it was safe now to face the truth.

'Where are they now?' she asked. 'Surely there must have been a trial—the police. . .' Her body was stiffening again. 'Why haven't I been questioned?'

'There was no point. The hospital knew when you came round from your coma that your memory had gone. And Sam was marvellous—I got him in straight away, I knew he was the man for you and he agreed with me that you mustn't be upset, you were in such a fragile state it could have sent you right over the edge. Questioning you, trying to make you remember, could have spelt disaster. And there was no need. My evidence was enough for the police.'

'You mean there's been a trial? You've been through all that, and I never knew?'

'No. Not yet. These things take time. The police are still preparing their case. But the men are safe enough,' he said quickly as she trembled suddenly in his arms. 'They're on remand—and they'll get heavy sentences. They'll never bother you again.'

Fenella nodded. Then she said quietly, 'I could give evidence now, though. Now that I've remembered.'

'You don't have to. Nobody will force you.'

'No,' she said, 'but I want to. I don't want you to go through all that alone.' They lay quietly for a while and again she marvelled that they could do this, lie naked in each other's arms without the flame of desire igniting between them. But it was as if they had come through some different consummation. As if the return of her memory had brought them together more closely, more deeply, than any physical expression could ever do.

She could remember now every detail of their previous relationship, every tiny, delicate stage in its growth. No wonder she had sometimes had that strange sense of familiarity, that feeling that she and Robert had known each other in some past, unknown life. It had been unknown only to her. . . She realised suddenly what it must have been like for him, living with her and knowing that she looked on him as a stranger. Feeling her hostility when they seemed unable to understand each other.

'Robert,' she said, aware that he had his own need of reassurance, 'I love you so much. I don't believe I ever stopped—even when I didn't know you. I kept having the strangest feelings—as if we'd met before, as if we knew each other on some deep, unknown level.'

'And so we did,' he said, wrapping his arms more tightly around her. 'But it was another kind of hell, waiting to see if you would ever remember me. And waiting to see whether, even if you didn't, the magic would work again. I was so afraid that your memory block wouldn't allow you to fall in love with me again.'

'Nothing could stop that,' she whispered. 'I fell in love with you very quickly, Robert. I wouldn't acknowledge it at first—I was so uncertain of anything I felt, groping my way. But in the end, I knew it. And when you kissed me—why did you go away then?'

'Because I was all too well aware of the effect that kiss had had on both of us. I knew that once we'd shared that kiss nothing could ever be the same again. We couldn't go back—we would have to go on. And it wasn't fair on you.' His tone was ragged as he relived the despair he had felt then. 'I wanted you to love me again—but I wanted you to love me as a whole man, not as a wheelchair-bound burden on you. That night, I felt I'd sunk to the lowest depths possible. I'd taken advantage of your vulnerability—I could, if I wanted, have you as my wife. And did I want it!' The emotion throbbed through his voice, quivered through his body. 'I nearly succumbed then, Fenella—I nearly asked you to marry me, to tie yourself to me for life, because I couldn't bear to live without you. But I couldn't quite do it. I knew that if I took you under those circumstances I'd despise myself for the rest of my life. And it would destroy us.'

Fenella was silent. She understood what he was saying, but she knew he was wrong—wrong, at least, as far as she was concerned. She would have accepted him willingly and with joy, without a thought for his disability. The thought that he might have taken advantage of her would never have entered her head. As far as she was concerned, the fact that they loved each other would have been enough.

But she could see that it was not the same for Robert. His male pride—his ego—would not have allowed him to offer her any less than his best. And even while she disagreed with his sentiment she valued it, and knew that this was an area in which they would never agree.

But it didn't matter. It was part of the essential difference between them. The difference between man and woman—the difference which brought all the magic that had coloured their relationship through two separate stages. Two distinct courtships, each with the same conclusion.

'Nothing could destroy us,' she said finally. 'Nothing could keep us apart. We're meant to be together, Robert.'

'Yes,' he said, and kissed her. 'I believe we are.' His lips returned to hers, with a growing passion that drew a gasp from her throat and brought her body, quivering, against his. 'I know we are. . .'

His mouth was on hers, covering her lips with tiny kisses then roving over her face, her eyelids, her ears and neck. Cupping one hand round her breast, he lifted it towards him and buried his lips in the softness, his fingertips caressing the crease below before straying further over her smooth, flat stomach. He splayed his fingers over her ribs, then down to her hip-bone and the straight, smooth line of her thigh; then he followed his fingers with lips that touched and burned with a tender fire that spread through every nerve.

'I love you very much,' he murmured, lifting himself so that his lips were against her ear. 'I wanted you to remember me—but now I want to rub out all those terrible memories forever. Will you let me?'

'You'll never rub them out now,' she whispered. 'They're a part of me, just as they're a part of you. And I want them, Robert. I want to know just what we've shared—the terrible times as well as the good. But you can rub out the horror—you can make me forget that in your arms. And, please. . . I want you to.'

'Fenella. . .' The name was no more than a sigh as he returned to a lovemaking that took her far beyond the stars. Tenderly, gently, he caressed her whole body, lingering over each sensitive area, stroking her shoulders, her spine, her feet and toes. Each caress he followed with a kiss, some as tiny and delicate as the touch of a butterfly's wing, some like fire on her quivering skin. He kissed her lips, her throat, her breasts, her stomach and hips, the tender skin of her thighs, her instep and each separate toe.

Fenella lay still, responding with tiny movements of each muscle as he touched it, whimpering softly as her senses reeled. Her body felt stretched taut, like a finely tuned musical instrument, and Robert was, with infinite and almost unbearably exciting tenderness, bringing her to a pitch at which she must experience the highest peak of sensation, or disintegrate entirely.

'Robert. . .' She whispered pleadingly, reaching down to let her fingers move in his thick hair. 'Robert. . .please. . .'

He raised himself against her, so that she could feel every hard, naked muscle against her shivering skin. Almost frantically, she sought his lips, clinging to him as he explored her mouth with sweet familiarity, and she knew that her body was telling him all that he needed to know, just as his was transmitting his need of her.

There was no need for words. Her clamouring emotions swept her away, lifting her against him in joyful surrender. With a groan as deep as a lion's purr, he caught her to him. And then they were together, their bodies in unison, moving in exquisite harmony that mounted to an almost intolerable delight before the night exploded and the stars showered around them.

'Course,' Mrs Bennett said as she handed round plates of delicious small sandwiches and sausage rolls, 'me and Walter always knew it was on the cards. I mean, you only had to look at them sometimes. . . And Miss Fenella—Mrs Milburn, I mean—was that upset when he went away.'

There were only a few guests. Sam, who had given Fenella away, looking like a particularly smartly dressed chimpanzee in his best suit; Andrew, who recovered quickly from any blow—and Fenella suspected that it hadn't been too severe a blow—to his own pride and had brought a very pretty girl called Marti from his office; Gina and her husband and sons, together with her brother through whom Robert had come to the party where he and Fenella had first met, and who was Robert's best man; some of the patients from the hospital and convalescent home, and a few people from Winchcombe and the surrounding area, who had known Robert most of his life.

They crowded round the newly married couple, wishing them well, and Fenella, looking at their smiling faces, felt warmed by their obvious sincerity. Everyone there was a friend, she thought, a true friend, in whom trust could be safely placed. She thought of her life through the past few years, her wanderings after Jeremy's betrayal and her parents' deaths. She remembered her panic when anyone had started to become too close to her. Man or woman, she'd never been able to trust—she'd always backed away, drawing back into her shell like a snail, when acquaintanceship had threatened to deepen into friendship, friendship into love.

Now she could see that her perception during those years had been distorted. Bitterly hurt by Jeremy's casual treatment of her, feeling cheapened and humiliated, she'd allowed her emotions to become twisted, had been unable to recognise truth when she saw it. Had been in danger of becoming permanently damaged—until Robert had come along, seen through the façade she'd erected around her, broken through the barrier and taught her to love again.

Perhaps it was no wonder that her mind had been unable to cope with any more trauma and had decided to close down on memories. But even that had not been able to withstand the power of the attraction between herself and Robert. She'd fallen in love with him all over again; the months when he had been away, with no word, had been like a desert. Oh, on the surface, she'd seemed happy enough—going out with Andrew or her new friends, spending companionable evenings at her flat. But all the time, deep down, she'd known this wasn't enough. All the time, she'd been yearning for Robert.

She moved across the room to his side, and, although he had his back to her, he seemed to know she was there. He turned and smiled down at her, lifting his glass of champagne in a silent toast.

'Happy?'

'What do you think?' she murmured. 'But I'll be even happier when we're alone.'

'Not long now.' He turned back to his conversation with a man who lived about ten miles away and had been a boyhood friend of Robert's. 'Yes, we're going skiing in January—Fenella's never tried before but I'm certain she's going to enjoy it. And it'll be extra special for me—taking her for the first time, as well as proving to that old sawbones over there just how wrong doctors can be.'

Sam heard the last remark and came over, a grin splitting his wizened face.

'And never more pleased to be wrong in my life,' he declared. 'But you have to remember that doctors are only human—and we can't gauge the power of the mind when it comes to overcoming disabilities. Many men would have spent the rest of their lives in their wheelchairs, with the injuries Robert had.'

'Well, look what an incentive I had to get better,' Robert said, and slipped his arm round Fenella's waist to draw her close to his side, while everyone raised their glasses and toasted the two of them.

At last everyone was gone and Mrs Bennett and the helpers she had recruited from the village— Sarah and another of the girls from the tea-shop— had tidied the room and disappeared to the kitchen. Feeling in need of a shower and change of clothes, Fenella went upstairs. She went into the big bedroom she had used before, and stood for a moment looking out of the window.

The Cotswold countryside lay spread before her, dusted with the first snow of the winter. The trees had lost their leaves and reached pencilled fingers into the sky; the old stone walls roamed across the fields, grey as the clouds above, rimed with a frosting of white. The golden walls and slate roofs of the town, just visible past the powerful turrets of the castle, were wreathed in wisps of smoke from fires that were being lit, and Fenella could imagine the cosy scenes inside those houses, with families preparing for tea and a quiet winter's evening together.

Turning away from the window, she went to the bathroom and showered. The warm spray ran down over her slender body and she stroked on gel, luxuriating in the scented steam.

'Why don't you let me do that?' Robert's voice said, and she opened her eyes.

He was standing naked by the shower door. Reaching up, he squeezed some gel into his palm and began to spread it over her body, his fingers slow and sensuous. Then he stepped inside and the spray enveloped them both, turning the gel into a soft foam that bubbled between them. Robert stroked it over her back, his arms wrapping themselves around her, and Fenella found her own arms slipping round his body as excitement and desire swept like a firestorm along every nerve.

'Well, Mrs Milburn?' he murmured deep in his throat. 'How do you think you'll enjoy married life?'

'I think I'll enjoy it very much,' Fenella whispered, and gasped as his fingers found a particularly sensitive spot, 'that's if I survive. . . Oh, Robert, Robert. . .'

'It's a little confined in here, don't you think?' He pressed his body against hers, slippery with gel and warm, sprinkling water. 'Perhaps we ought to get out before we drown—hmm? What do you think?'

'I think I've already drowned.' Her senses were

reeling and she could barely stand as Robert stepped away. With a swift movement, he turned off the water and then lifted her in his arms. He carried her across to the bed and laid her down. Dimly, she realised that he must have already spread it with towels; their thick softness rubbed gently against her skin and she smiled at the practical streak which always marched with the romantic in this man she had married.

His body shining as if it had been oiled, Robert knelt beside her and began once again that long, tender exploration which she found so arousing. With expert fingers, with lips that brought fire to each pore, he caressed her skin until no particle of it was left neglected. And only when she lay shivering, her blood singing, her body scorched by his touch, did he stretch himself beside her and allow her to feel his own warm skin and begin her own exploration.

'No hurry,' he murmured as she pressed close against him, 'no hurry. We've got the rest of our lives to love each other, my darling. The rest of our lives.' He turned suddenly and took her face between his hands, laying his lips on hers in a kiss that it seemed would never end. 'I love you, Fenella.'

'And I love you,' she said. And was thankful then for all those memories, for she would not have missed a moment of their loving; neither the first time, nor the second.

Deep in her heart, she knew she had never really forgotten his love.

Accept 4 Free Romances and 2 Free gifts

• FROM MILLS & BOON •

An irresistible invitation from Mills & Boon Reader Service. Please accept our offer of 4 free romances, a CUDDLY TEDDY and a special MYSTERY GIFT... Then, if you choose, go on to enjoy 6 more exciting Romances every month for just £1.45 each postage and packaging free. Plus our FREE newsletter with author news, competitions and much more.

Send the coupon below at once to:
Reader Service, FREEPOST, P.O. Box 236, Croydon, Surrey CR9 9EL

✂ — — — — ┤ NO STAMP NEEDED ├ — — — —

YES! Please rush me my 4 Free Romances and 2 FREE Gifts! Please also reserve me a Reader Service Subscription so I can look forward to receiving 6 Brand New Romances each month for just £8.70, post and packing free. If I choose not to subscribe I shall write to you within 10 days. I understand I can keep the free books and gifts whatever I decide. I can cancel or suspend my subscription at any time. I am over 18 years of age.

Name Mr/Mrs/Miss _____ EP86R

Address _____

_____

_____ Postcode _____

Signature _____

Mills & Boon

Next month's Romances

Each month, you can choose from a world of variety in romance with Mills & Boon. These are the new titles to look out for next month.

WHEN THE DEVIL DRIVES Sara Craven

PAYMENT DUE Penny Jordan

LAND OF DRAGONS Joanna Mansell

FLIGHT OF DISCOVERY Jessica Steele

LEAVE LOVE ALONE Lindsay Armstrong

THE DEVIL'S KISS Sally Wentworth

THE IRON MASTER Rachel Ford

BREAKING THE ICE Kay Gregory

STEPS TO HEAVEN Sally Heywood

A FIERY ENCOUNTER Margaret Mayo

A SPECIAL SORT OF MAN Natalie Fox

MASTER OF MARSHLANDS Miriam Macgregor

MISTAKEN LOVE Shirley Kemp

BROKEN DREAMS Jennifer Williams

STOLEN KISSES Debbie Macomber

STARSIGN
DOUBLE DECEIVER Rebecca King

Available from Boots, Martins, John Menzies, W.H. Smith, Woolworths and other paperback stockists.

Also available from Mills and Boon Reader Service, P.O. Box 236, Thornton Road, Croydon, Surrey CR9 3RU.